LOVER

Short Stories by Harriet Zinnes

Coffee House Press :: Minneapolis :: 1988

Some of these stories were originally published in *Ararat, Bloodroot, Carleton Miscellany, Chance Music, Croton Review, Gallimaufry, Mundus Artium, North Dakota Quarterly, Phoebe, Primavera, Pulp, Red Weather,* and *Valhala* 7, to whose editors grateful acknowledgement is made. "Marie, Marie, Hold on Tight," originally appeared in *New Directions* 30, copyright © 1975; "Pure Will" in *Solo: Women on Women Alone,* copyright © 1977 (Leo Hamalian, ed.: New York, Laurel & Delacorte); "Cosmetic Instrument" in *New Directions* 42, copyright © 1981; "Wings" in *New Directions in Prose and Poetry* 52, copyright © 1988. These four stories are used by permission of their respective publishers.

Back cover photo by Stella Snead.

The writer wishes to express her gratitude to the MacDowell Colony, the Virginia Center for the Creative Arts, and Yaddo for periods of residency during which she worked on some of the stories in this volume.

The publisher thanks the following organizations whose support helped make this book possible: The National Endowment for the Arts, a federal agency; The Jerome Foundation; and United Arts.

Coffee House Press books are distributed to the trade by Consortium Book Sales and Distribution, 213 East Fourth Street, Saint Paul, Minnesota 55101. Our books are also available through all major library distributors and jobbers, and through most small press distributors, including Bookpeople, Bookslinger, Inland, Pacific Pipeline, and Small Press Distribution. For personal orders, catalogs, or other information, write to Coffee House Press, 27 North Fourth Street, Suite 400, Minneapolis, Mn 55401.

Library of Congress Cataloging in Publication Data
Zinnes, Harriet.
Lover : Short stories / by Harriet Zinnes.
p. cm.
ISBN 0-918273-46-3 (alk. paper) : $9.95
1. Love stories, American. I. Title.
PS3576.I56L68 1989
813'.54–DC19 89-862

Contents

TWO ROADS / 1

WINGS / 4

MARIE, MARIE, HOLD ON TIGHT / 9

PACT / 11

YES, DEAR JOHN / 21

BELLOWS / 30

STARS, ETC. / 34

VIRGINIA FARM / 40

BLACK SNAKE / 42

COSMETIC INSTRUMENT / 48

ELOQUENCE / 54

POOLSIDE / 63

GROPE / 68

DE L'ESSENCE / 70

PICASSO'S GOAT / 72

ANCIENT RITUAL / 85

SHE WASN'T JOYCE'S NORA / 89

AT THE WHITNEY: A DIALOGUE / 98

GREEN CATERPILLAR / 102

NO RABBITS / 107

PURE WILL / 110

NUN'S STORY / 112

DISCIPLE / 115

GRAVEN IMAGE / 117

LOVER / 125

"I AM NOT I ANY LONGER WHEN I SEE"/129

LOST / 133

UPTIGHT / 135

THE ROOM / 139

For Eric

Two Roads

It is ten o'clock in the morning. The air is fresh and lovely. The sun high up tantalizingly clear. It is morning. It is the kind of morning to meet a lover. She showers in the cold water. Suds all over her body. A clear body a clear morning. A morning to meet a lover. She dresses. Goes downstairs. A croissant. A coffee. It is not Paris, but if it is a morning to meet a lover it must be like Paris. Now it is in the country. In America. In New England. The air is fresh and lovely, and she has showered and had croissants, and now it is a morning to meet a lover. She puts on an Irish sweater. It is still cool in this morning that is not Paris but like Paris because the air is fresh and lovely and it is cool and she has taken a cold shower and now she is ready. Ready to meet her lover in New England where she has had croissants (frozen of course but baked in an oven, an old oven a 100-year-old oven that is black and has a chimney and you have to stir the fire with a poker). She is thirty years old and that is old in New York but not in Paris and not in New England where it does not matter. She is slight and her breasts are taut and her hair shiny, and she has a tinkle of a laugh and her teeth are white and it is clear this morning that she is meeting her lover. Her glowing face her silky hair her hips that move and say *I am I am I am I will love I will love I will love you who will know the poppies and lilacs of my body* who will eat the rose of this summer morning today in New England.

But it is morning a morning to meet a lover and she is dressed in her Irish sweater and she is ready. She walks out of the house with the broad door that has a keyhole that is long and narrow and has a key like the French ones heavy and solid and like the Americans of long ago because this is a keyhole in an American house of long ago with a gabled roof and a wooden porch and old rockers with wicker seats and the legs are chipped and the rocking unstable but it is lovely to sit on the porch in early evening where the logs for the fire are stacked and there are promises of fires slow burning fires to read by and before which many a young and many an old person has read.

It is morning a morning to meet a lover and she is dressed in her Irish sweater and she is off. Down the long road where there are yarrow and ferns and purple vetch not a bit pretty but crude and promising and she is walking where the moles are hidden no rabbits cross her path and the foxes in the woods are out of sight. She walks down the lonely road and she is not lonely. She is walking to meet her lover in the morning that is fresh and lovely and it is summer.

It is summer and she is walking down the road to meet her lover and the riot bombs of Boston are holes in her memory and the pebbles on the road are tokens of love and she is walking on the road with her Irish sweater and her arms are free and she is wearing a hat the hat that she wore when he and she when the week before they had played tennis all morning and had gone to the lake and swum in the nude and gone to her home and made love in a bed that was in a room where the windows were low and the sun streamed in and they sipped their sherry and said the words that were old but not dreary and they did the things that her body suggested today this day as she walked down the road to meet her lover who would greet her with smiles who would say the words that she longed to hear that she knew were as old as the vetch on the road and as young as the yarrow and the fern and the rabbits that were hidden and the moles that were certain to lie in their beds in the ground that had felt the footsteps of long ago on the ground that was careless and free and certain of the years of rain and of water certain of feet that would follow through ages that would hold the footsteps in sands so tiny that the footsteps would mingle with the stones and the shadows that were cast even then by the branches of trees that had lived for at least half a century and had felt the wind of an equal time and said nothing to her as she passed down the road to meet her lover in the morning that was fresh and lovely and crisp in an air that said *Come come into the house the house of your lover* who has sherry and words and a body that bristles with the tune of desire that empties itself as if it were the river that does not cross the road she is walking but that is there in his body that will flow in her own and will marry her to the song of the summer and her heart will keep time with the beat of her ears that will hear the measures of the birds that are singing and her heart will beat with her steps on the path she is going going on going on to meet with her lover this morning when the air is fresh and lovely where there is no river but the river of her longing.

Wings

He opened the door and saw the chair in the center of the little room. He was surprised of course. What visitor had displaced that chair, his Eames chair that never, simply never was moved from in front of his desk? He looked quickly around the room to see whether anything else had been moved. Had his apartment been broken into? He walked over to the desk itself, quickly glanced at his books and typewriter, then opened the top drawer, shut that, opened the drawers on the side. Nothing touched. Nothing seemingly removed. He walked over to the large filing cabinet and again opened drawers. Again everything in place. He left what he called his study—a mere anteroom really—and walked into the living room. Had he raised the lid of his grand piano? He couldn't remember doing that. He looked at the couch, not at all disheveled, the chairs, the little tables, lamps in order. He again walked over to the piano. He was sure John had left his Schubert notes on the ledge of the piano. Wasn't he in the midst of rehearsing? And what was Satie's *Gnossienne* doing opened on the piano bench? He went into the dining room, glanced at the neat buffet, and then opened the drawers of the little chest in which he kept his mother's silver. Everything in place.

He then walked into his bedroom. Walked directly to his bureau to look at the drawers of his chest, especially the top drawer where he kept gold cufflinks, tie pins, and those silly gold chains that he never wore but that his first love Ted Blight had given him. As he was opening the drawer, a strange voice called out to him: "Hi." He turned abruptly, his heart pounding. What he saw was more a little girl than a woman. A twelve-year-old girl (or was she a woman?) was sitting propped up on pillows. His pillows! She kept staring at him, smiling, holding him transfixed, as she casually took out a cigarette lighter and lit a cigarette. "Smoke?" she asked.

"I never smoke in my bedroom–and don't allow anyone else to," he found himself saying sharply.

She smiled at that. "Rule No. 1 just broken."

Why didn't he retort to that or at least walk over to her, even run over, and grab the cigarette from her mouth? He was certainly capable of doing a thing like that, especially under the anger he was feeling. "I wish you'd put out that cigarette," he found himself saying quietly.

"Oh, I'm not going to do that. I always smoke in bedrooms, especially the bedrooms of the men whom I have followed."

"Followed? You've been following me?" He was stunned. Had he been so preoccupied lately about the play's possible closing that he was not aware when he was being followed? "How long have you been following me? And for god's sake why? Why have you been following me?"

"One question at a time. I've been following you since I saw you perform in *Oh! Calcutta,* and I've been following you because I like you. This morning you happened to have left your apartment door open–I gather you were late for your rehearsal–so that it was easy enough for me to get in."

"Left my apartment door open? I'm becoming absentminded. But how long have you been following me?"

"Three days. You see, it didn't take long to trap you."

"Trap me? Yes, that's it exactly. You have trapped me. Now that you are here holding me entrapped, as it were, hm, now what do you want of me? May I sit down at least?" Why on earth was he asking her permission? She wasn't holding him at gunpoint. Merely with her eyes, and that god-awful cigarette. "Will you leave now, now that you have made your presence known and have found me in my own apartment? Surely that is all you want. You may get off the bed now, thank you."

"But that's exactly where I want to be. You are an idiot. Why do you suppose I've been following you if I didn't want to get into bed with you. Why?"

"You don't want to go to bed with me," he blurted out with astonishment. "Not with me. Don't you know, don't you know I don't like women!"

"I know," she said calmly, "but I like you and there's no reason after all why you can't be trained to like me. I'm not that ugly, and at first I'll make very few demands on you. I've trained men like you before. You'll be all right. Don't worry. You may be my chief star. You may require only one lesson. Come here. Let's start our first session. It may be the last, really. Don't be shy. I won't hurt you."

He couldn't believe that he was walking toward the bed. What kind of witch was she? Not only did he walk over to the bed – the wrong side; he never slept on that side of the bed with his lovers – but he began to undress: took off his shoes, his socks, his jacket, shirt, tie, undershirt (that gorgeous pink one that Al so loved) and finally with just a little embarrassment his undershorts, pink bikinis, hot pink of course, with that daring scarlet red border.

"You're doing just fine," she said soothingly. "I'll start by giving you an encouraging kiss." Shivering, he accepted that light kiss. It was on his cheek, thank goodness, he thought. Why was he shivering, and why wasn't he running away? Why wasn't he throwing her forcibly off the bed?

"Look here," he found himself saying, "I don't want any more of your entrapment. I don't like women, and surely not little girls – are you twelve or thirteen, for heaven's sake – and this is my bed, my apartment, my life. Why why don't you get out of here, once and for all?" But his actions were belying his words. Imagine. He was kissing her on the lips and he thought he heard all sorts of mad words such as *darling dear sweetheart my love.* Whatever was happening here in his own bedroom? He wasn't chagrined or mortified. Maybe he was on the stage and just simply did not know where he was. He remembered his part in that Shaw play in which he was wooing that older woman. What was the name of the play? Wasn't he called Eugene or something like that? Maybe he was now on stage. "Are we rehearsing a play? Say, are we rehearsing a play? Tell me, what's my part like? Am I getting the leading role? Whom am I playing opposite? You're not my leading lady, are you? And what is your name? And how old are you anyway?"

At this point he recognized she had no energy for words. She was forcing him to enter her, and he was doing just that. Did the director call for the act itself? Oh god, wasn't he in a Broadway production? Was it just porn? Had he been shot into the twenty-first century where such things were permitted on the legitimate stage? What country was he in, what stage, what city, and above all, what play–and did he have the leading role? But he suddenly felt himself spent, and threw himself off the little girl–surely she was just a little girl–and stretched out his arms across the bed. "You little witch," he said without any animosity, "you've tired me out: and I don't believe it, yes, you've given me pleasure. But what play are we in, what play?"

As he picked himself up and turned to her side of the bed, he was appalled that she wasn't there. Of course she's probably gone to the john. He waited for what seemed at least ten minutes. He hardly had the strength to get off the bed to look for her. At first he decided to call out. But what was her name? "Little girl," he began, "little girl, where are you? Are you in the john? Come out, will you? I've got to ask you more questions." No answer. "Little girl," he called again. "Where are you?" Still no answer. He'd just have to pick himself up off the bed and investigate. Entirely nude (and he never let his lovers see him nude: it was his rule NEVER TO BE TOTALLY REVEALED) he walked toward the bathroom. The door was wide open. She was not there. He made a frantic tour of the apartment. She was nowhere to be seen. Should he try to run out to find her? Without his clothes? That would never do. No, he'd better run into his room and dress quickly for the pursuit. He was dashing into his room toppling his best marble table and adorable Tiffany lamp when the crash of the lamp called him to his senses. *But this is my opportunity to get rid of her. What am I doing trying to find her? Am I so bewitched that I can't even know when I have it good?* Trembling – still with the shock of his new delight and with the equally new discovery that he could get rid of a strange creature who had bewitched him, he sat down entirely naked on his favorite leather chair, snuggled up in it, and tried to recover his senses. The only action surely was inaction. He came quickly to that conclusion. His brain apparently had not been harmed. He could think straight and hard. That little witch had followed him and had had him. He had surely been had. And it was over. Relieved he felt his back arch comfortably against the chair. He was just about to close his eyes with exhaustion and triumph, when he heard a small voice say, "Bye-bye my love. You were beautiful."

He looked up in time to see the little girl spread wings and fly directly out of his living room window. Luckily it's a French window, he thought. John was right when he chose that.

Marie, Marie, Hold on Tight

HERE IT IS ten o'clock and the man who delivers the eggs has not appeared. He is usually so sallow that it is probably best he has the eggs in that white box. Even white eggs can look rusty yellow when a man in a long dirty white coat with a sagging face delivers them. Why I accept his deliveries I don't know. I don't even eat the eggs. I don't even cook the eggs. I don't even throw them away. I suppose Marie takes them. What other recompense does she have? I give her no money. She never asks for any. And is it right for me to be so crude as to suggest the need of lucre? Money. It is dirty yellow too. Marie likes bright colors. Every red or green dress I had she has taken. I have only blacks and whites left. She is selective. And she ought to be–with clothes, that is. She doesn't care about her men. Even the plumber, that fat, crooked-nosed, partly crippled man gives her titillations. I hear her giggle when he decides to take the rod, that long snakelike thing, to repair a stopped-up sink. She manages to get close to him, too. Asking silly questions. As if she cares whether or not her combings have stopped the sink. And he listens with that sly wink. Who knows what she does when she says good-by. She takes her time about it. When he comes I never seem to get my tea. And the toast is always burned that day. Maybe with the egg man too. Maybe that's why he's late. Maybe she's with him now. "Marie! Marie!"

Here it is ten o'clock and the man who delivers the eggs has not appeared. And I'm wearing Madame's low-cut red dress too, the one with the big bow at the place he likes so much. Such big hands he has. So much warmer than the plumber's, and quick too. He knows how to make me jump. It's good he comes in the morning. When I can get to that perfume and douse myself with it so when he takes off that dirty white coat and places his pants (neatly too!) on the chair (lucky he hates underwear) he can hold me tight and do it to me standing up so that I think I'll faint with pleasure – and we have to be so quiet too. Oh but what a nuisance is Madame, with her "Marie! Marie!" Does she know anything? What did that husband of hers ever do to *her* before she became an invalid. I wish I could have seen him. I'd give him his pleasures! I bet *his* was as big as that egg man's. At least his picture says all kinds of swishy bed things. I'd make him discover *me*. But I'm not doing too bad here: eggs all over me, and services of all kinds delivered here and to *me*. "Marie! Marie!" There she goes again.

Here it is ten o'clock and I'm still in my truck and I won't deliver the eggs. What eggs? I haven't any more to deliver. You'd think I gave Marie enough. Does she use eggs too? Insatiable that girl is. Insatiable. She tires me out. She thinks I'm a machine. An egg machine! Maybe I'll get her a pigeon. Pigeons make eggs and eggs make pigeons and pigeons make love too. And what about Madame. How long will she remain dumb? Or doesn't she care? I've heard stories. She knows too much. Her eyes can give a man the what-for. She just sits in her chair doing nothing. Doesn't look at TV or read a book or knit. She doesn't even gossip. But those eyes of hers giving me . . . Is it a come-on? Yeah, her husband was a colonel. Those army wives. Maybe it is the come-on she's giving me. With her sallow face. Her long dirty white dress. And Marie says she doesn't even eat eggs. Poison, she says. Poison. Maybe I can meet her on her own terms. NO EGGS.

Pact

WHEN SHE WENT to put the hat on her daughter's head, she stopped short. She found herself holding the hat in both hands, drawn to her lips. She was frightened. The little girl merely stood waiting to be finally dressed for the drive to the party. Her daughter's motionless wait made her panicky. Slowly she removed the hat and her hands from her lips and motioned to the girl to come toward her. The girl obeyed quickly. She placed the hat with a single firm motion on the girl's head. Picking up her shawl from the chair, she threw it around her shoulders and grabbed the girl's hand. The hand lay limply in her own. She shuddered.

"My God, we've forgotten Charlie's present."

"Oh. Where did we put it, Mommy?"

"On my dresser, Mary. I think the envelope with the card is scotch-taped to it, too."

The girl ran up the stairs toward the bedroom, her first lively motion of the day. The mother was cold. She hugged the shawl more closely around her shoulders. She was glad she was wearing woolen pants rather than jeans. Soon the girl was back with the gift. She was smiling. "I had to scotch-tape it myself," she said. Her eyes shone.

"You did it well. Very well," the mother said, examining the envelope. "We had better rush. We are late. It was supposed to begin at twelve-thirty, you know. A lunch party. I bet you'll have hamburgers and pickles. And potato chips, too."

The girl said nothing. Her mother thought she noticed the child's lips twitch.

"I want to sit in the back," Mary said on reaching the car.

"All right, but be sure to push down the button on the door."

Silence all the way to Charlie's house. Ten minutes of it. "Don't come in," the girl said. "Parents never do at Charlie's." Should she fight? "All right. Have a good time. I'll call for you at four unless Mrs. Parker calls me to come earlier." She winced–Mary was out of earshot. She never gave me a good-by kiss. A long sigh. A start of the motor. The short drive. The car in the garage. The key in the door. The walk up the stairs to the bedroom. "I hate this shawl," Corinne said aloud as she threw it on the bed and plopped herself down on it. For a second she thought she would cry. Her chest felt heavy. Tears seemed to bubble under her lids. But she did not cry. She picked up a copy of *The New Yorker* and read a long poem by somebody or other about fruits and vegetables. It was boring. Suddenly she hated fruits. She hated vegetables. And particularly poems about them.

She tried not to dwell on Mary's remorselessly cold behavior toward her. She knew it had to do with the divorce. But why bother examining the cause of it. It was there. She was here. It was all so unnerving. Wasn't it bad enough that Ted had left? Why was she always receiving the punishment. His little girl too. But of course only his every-other-weekend little girl. Otherwise hers hers hers twenty-four hours of the day. I wish I could cry. She picked up the magazine again. Her eyes began to tear. She let the tears fall down on the poem about fruits and vegetables.

When the telephone rang, she woke up. It must have been ringing for some time. "Yes? Oh, Mrs. Parker. Yes, of course. I'll pick her up. Sorry I'm late. I'll be there in ten minutes." *What a sharp-tongued Mrs. Parker. Of course I shouldn't have slept through four. But it's only four-thirty. You'd think . . .*

Mary was waiting for her near the curb, her cheeks flushed, obviously controlling excitement. She was holding something wobbling in her hand, red and blue. The girl jumped into the back seat, said nothing. "How was the party, Mary? Did you have the hamburger?" No reply. "Were there good games? Prizes?"

"I won a Raggedy Ann doll." "You did? Hold it up so I can see it in the mirror? I thought I saw you holding something nice."

"I love it. I love it." Mary *loved* something. Something had happened. "I guess you have to call her Raggedy. Right? Or will you name it something else."

"Raggedy Raggedy Raggedy. Her name's Raggedy," Mary chanted, hugging the doll. "Now we have another member of the family. Great." Corinne was sorry she said that, sorry to remind Mary of her loss. Raggedy was no substitute for Daddy.

The car in the garage. The key in the door. "Let's hang up your coat, Mary. And do give me your hat."

"Yes, take it. I hate the hat. Why did you put it on me? I don't want to wear it again. Ever ever." Mary had run up the stairs. Her door banged shut. The hat. The hat. There must be something about the hat, I felt it too, Corinne thought. A hat covers; it traps the head in. OK. No more hat. She took it with her to the kitchen and with extreme care placed her foot on the pedal of the garbage can, saw the cover raised, and pushed the hat deep down into the bin. No more hat. First pushed down on head. Then pushed down into bin. No more hat.

The telephone rang. It was Ted. "I'm calling you early. Listen, I can't have Mary next weekend. I've got to go out of town. There's a convention. OK?" A convention. Of course not a weekend with Patty. Oh no. Why can't he be honest even now. We've been divorced for two years, after all. "Hope this won't spoil your plans too much." But even if she had had plans he knew she, the mother, the old sow, would have to break them. What would she do? Place Mary in an orphanage or something for the weekend? His Patty weekend? "Should I place Mary in an orphanage?" she heard herself saying. "What did you say? What in hell do you mean, 'orphanage'?" "I said of course Mary can stay with me. *I said, the child can stay with me,*" she shouted. "Oh. She can stay with you. Good. Give her my love, will you?" Of course. He never asks about me. *My* love. What is that anyway? He knows I have no love. No love no love. Corinne hung up. No good-by kiss either.

Raggedy was settled in. Mary had taken out all of her dolls from the head of the crib, and with great care had propped Raggedy against the pillow. She put the dolls at Raggedy's feet. *You are the queen! And you have no king, you poor thing, you poor thing.* Raggedy seemed consolable. But Mary sighed deeply. She puttered around the crib, tucking in Raggedy, despairing of her ever keeping dry, and deciding quite improperly to give her a bath directly after her feeding. And then it was again tucking in here, tucking in there, and then the final fluffing of pillow and the beginning of the fairy tale for the night. She read her the story of Rapunzel, and then set Raggedy on the outer window sill and pretended to comb the knobby hair. It was all over much too soon. Mother was calling her to come to dinner, and her own bedtime was near. Nights were even more dreadful than the days, she told Raggedy, who she felt understood completely, for Raggedy too had no father to tuck her in.

Mary helped with the dishes. She had been doing that since she was six, and at eight she continued quite routinely to gather them up from the table and scrub them gently with the brush before placing them in the dishwasher. Corinne thought she'd broach the weekend disaster while they did the cleaning up. "Daddy's going to a convention. This Friday night."

"Oh."

"Yes. For the weekend."

"With Patty?"

"Oh, I don't know." Already jealous. But not for Mom, oh no, for herself. "Probably alone. It's business, you know."

"I was going to show him Raggedy. Now he won't see her for three weeks."

"Maybe next weekend. I'm sure next weekend.'

"I don't think so. Three weeks. It'll be three weeks."

Corinne saw the tears welling up in Mary's eyes. She walked over to the girl to hug her. "Don't touch me," Mary shouted as she bolted from the room and ran up the stairs to her bedroom. The door banged shut. Always the door banged shut.

Mary was right. Ted did not take Mary the next weekend. He kept to a calculated arithmetic–every other week, despite cancellations. Did he really love Mary? But he loved Patty more?

Patty was included in the weekend. They were going to the Central Park Zoo and then for the inevitable chocolate at Rumpelmayer's. Mary sipped her chocolate quietly there, looking straight at Patty with her long hair, her opal skin, and her terribly thin body. "Why is she so thin," she had once asked her father. She knew her mother was not thin and thought that was to her advantage. Her father seemed puzzled, as if he had never thought about the subject. "Is she thin? Too thin? All young women are thin. You'll be too when you grow up." "Oh no. I'll be like Mommy. I'll have a round face and laughing eyes. You always said I have Mommy's laughing eyes. Patty doesn't at all. They're so narrow! And her lashes are so long. Are they false, Daddy?"

But they are at Rumpelmayer's now, and Daddy is looking at Patty and smiling and Mary is looking at Patty and frowning and Patty is looking at Mary and scolding: "Why aren't you wearing your hat, Mary, in this cold December weather? It looks like snow, too. You had such a pretty one when I last saw you. Why didn't you wear it today?"

Mary's lips twitched. Daddy noticed and patted her hand. "I'm sure Mary just didn't want a hat today. And besides, look how lovely her hair looks when the wind turns it this way and that." And he became the wind ruffling her hair this way and that. Mary loved his wind.

Patty just said: "How strange your mother was so careless."

"My mother's not careless. She listens to me." Tears were in Mary's eyes. She hoped she wouldn't cry. She didn't. Daddy saved her. "Patty, forget the hat, please." Mary knew it wouldn't be hard. Often Patty completely disregarded her. Even at Rumpelmayer's. Then Mary would look around at the other tables and feel sympathy for all the children there, even though she was sure that most were with real grandmothers or mothers or aunts and some even with real mothers and fathers. But it was awful there. And she was sure all the children felt the same way that she did. Once, a boy her age, with a white tennis sweater in the early fall, had smiled at her. Smiled at her as if he were Charlie. She liked Rumpelmayer's then. But she never saw him again. Would she ever see a boy who . . . Boys were funny. Like her daddy. If she had only had a brother.

"Daddy, why didn't you and Mother ever have a boy. Why didn't I ever have a brother. Charlie has a sister, though she's a horror. But Charlie's really nice."

"Well, you may have a stepbrother some day, mayn't she, Patty? How would you like that?"

"I'd hate it hate it. He would be a baby, and anyway he'd never be around except I suppose I might see him every other weekend. Maybe." She looked hard at her father whose eyes turned to Patty's out of embarrassment, or was it love? Mary hated Patty then more than ever. A stepbrother. Ugh.

"Anyway, there's no immediate danger, Mary. Don't you like your chocolate cake? You're not eating it. No, you're not eating it. Do." Patty's voice was sharp. Her narrow pointed nose seemed like a sword. Mary dreamt once of simply cutting it off. But it never worked, not even in the dream. She couldn't find the proper knife.

Suddenly, Mary remembered Raggedy. "I forgot to tell you, Daddy. I won a prize at Charlie's birthday party. A Raggedy Ann doll."

"Marvelous. Is it a big or little one?"

"Medium size, I think." Mary cupped her hands to indicate the size.

"You'll probably take it to college with you."

Was Patty being mean? You could never tell with Patty. She could be so hateful.

"College? What a funny idea."

Daddy was on Mary's side.

"A mascot, silly. College girls have loads of Raggedy Ann dolls around their rooms. Once at Vassar a girl who majored in art made a painting of her Raggedy. In fact, she made a series of paintings of her Raggedy. What do you think of that, Mary?"

Mary ignored Patty's question and wished she had not even mentioned the doll. She wouldn't even show it to her father when he brought her home. Home. She'd like that right now. But would she really? Her mother never laughing anymore. And she knew she was cruel to her, but she couldn't stand her eyes watching her all the time, her fussing, as if she expected her to cry for her daddy every minute. She knew it was her mother who had the tears all the time. Anyway, why did Mommy let him go? To Patty. Why why? It was that night when she had heard her mother crying and screaming, yes, screaming. Never had she heard her scream before. But her father said nothing. Nothing. What was he doing while Mommy was crying? Why didn't he say something? Why did her mother shout so and say those words that she tried hard to forget. She even heard them once in a nightmare: *get out get out get out of here and never come back never come back.* She knew now why she had said those horrid things. Charlie had told her, and he was right–it was because of Patty. Patty had been there right along and Daddy had been yes "unfaithful." And he is unfaithful now too, to me. Mommy is sad and I am sad, and Raggedy is sad. Only Charlie's sister is not sad. Quite clearly not sad. Patty is sad too. I know she is sad. She is so mean. Daddy is not sad. The only one not sad. Why is Daddy not sad? I must ask Charlie. Charlie would know. He's nine now. Nine. I'll be nine in June. Not too far away. But I'll go far away. Yes, they'll send me far away. To northern Ontario. To a camp. I'll hate it. Charlie won't be there. I'll take Raggedy. Will the girls laugh at me? Will they think me too old for Raggedy? But if the girls take Raggedy to Vassar . . .

"I'll be back on Wednesday, though," Patty was saying. Daddy seemed hurt. "Why do you have to leave? Your mother doesn't actually need you. She's been sick before and you were perfectly content to remain here. St. Louis is far away."

Daddy's being hurt now. Will he be sad too? He ought to be sad.

"If I remain, will you go to Sanibel?"

Oh, she's foxy. Will Daddy be taken in?

"Great God, girl, I work, you know. I can't just pick myself up and leave the office. Besides, there's that godawful new manuscript that just came in. A helluva editing job."

Mary wanted to go home. Patty looked at Daddy.

"I have to go to St. Louis."

"Daddy, I want to go home."

"St. Louis it will be, then. And home, too, Mary."

There were things to resolve and yet nothing to resolve. Corinne fidgeted with her hands. Maybe she should think of redecorating the house. She looked at the shabby couch with its fading beige corduroy cover, and the flokati rug that had long since lost its fluff. She looked at the buffet in the dining room, remembering when they had bought it, with Ted's first big raise. She hated it now, hated it. It was so narrow, and there was never even room enough to make a proper buffet dinner. She was still dragging things in and out of the kitchen. Maybe she ought to have a dinner party just the same. For whom? Not for Ted's old friends. Or hers who after these two years were still pretending to help. Even the divorced ones. Urging her to go to singles' bars. Or clubs. Or worse yet, those singles' weekends. Sally suggested the New School. That seemed the best idea, even if Ted taught there once a week. She could avoid that day. What would she study? Writing? My god, compete with Ted? Family Relationships? Freud and the Film? The Jungian Archetype As Seen Through the Shape of the Belly Button? Maybe The Women's Movement and Men's Impotence? Or the course about The Course That the Watergate Scandal Took Before Nixon Resigned. Linotyping. That might be the best of all. How to Start Your Own Press and Win a Guggenheim. Oh crap. She might as well take up knitting.

Mary decided her mother was at least faithful, even though she poked around and watched her every move. She would switch allegiances. Just like that. It would be mother, not father. Daddy could go to all the conventions he liked. With or without Patty. And Patty could go to Vassar with her own mascot. Or to Sani... wherever. And she would call Charlie to tell him about it. Her switch. And she would get back her hat and let her mother cover her head, smack it right down on her head. Her hat would be the pact between them. Daddy was saying good-by. Of course he couldn't do anything but drop her off. No Raggedy Ann for him. "Good-by Daddy. Thank you." "Good-by Mary. Say hello to Mommy." No good-by to Patty who turned her head. A good-by kiss to Daddy.

Mommy was sitting in the kitchen, her hands on her lap. Were there tears in her eyes? Probably. Mary walked over to her and kissed her cheek. "Mary! How sweet! Did you have fun? Was it Rumpelmayer's again?"

Mary said yes. Mary said yes. Mary said: "Mommy, I missed my hat."

"What hat? Patty said something about a hat in December, didn't she."

"Oh no. I just missed the hat. I'll put it on when I go to school tomorrow."

"But why on earth this yen for the hat, Mary? I threw it out."

"You . . ."

"Yes, threw it out. You didn't like it. You said you even hated it. I thought you'd be glad."

"Oh." The pact was broken. No hat. "But you wanted me to wear the hat."

"But not if you didn't want it. Really not. Are you angry that I threw it out?"

"Oh, I had hoped you'd be able to put on the hat when I went to school tomorrow."

"But why, for heaven's sake? What's so important about the hat?"

What *was* so important about the hat? She could make another pact. "If you don't have the hat, then, well, what would you like me to do?"

"To do?"

"To do to make you happy."

Yes, Dear John

It is in the early evening, the stars still invisible. Little Mary is already asleep in the house. John is looking at the vegetable garden, poking around the cucumbers in the half dark. Margaret sits in the hammock alone. Place, place. Perhaps place really matters. Maybe were I in Connecticut looking at the tobacco rows, I'd feel different. Or do persons matter more. John near me, Mary sleeping in her bed upstairs. Do they really matter. Make me more or less myself, the other. Have I become ME. Does it really matter? Matter? The earth the matter, the vegetable garden – the only matter?

"Look, Marge. Come quickly." John's voice, his eager voice. Always seeing something. How can he be so curious? Is it a worm, even a new kind of fly with a bright green belly or a chipmunk, quiet, waiting.

"Marge, come quickly. Come quickly. Oh forget it, it's gone." Of course it's gone. Come quickly, go quickly. Nothing lasts. What does it matter if it does not last. Last last. The last on the shoe, the last time John's kiss really mattered. How can she be so changed, so cool when she is only thirty. If she's so cool now what will happen . . .

"Why didn't you come when I called, Marge. You're always missing the most important adventure of the day. I saw a . . ."

"Oh cut it. I really don't care tonight for your bugs and worms and new shoots. I really want to be alone. Really, John I want..."

"OK. I'll leave you here. I'm walking over to Lou's. We're going to have a game of poker. Some beer. Shall I send Kathy over?"

"Of course not. I want to be alone, I said."

Marge watches John's long thin body make strides that in the old days excited her as she tried to keep pace with him in their walks. Then she loved to hear him identify the flowers and trees, while his sensitive hands made arcs, encompassing his meaningful world, and his long blond hair triumphed in the sun. She could hardly stand it then, so near him, walking. She could hardly listen to him. She wanted to be close close, to have him hold her tightly. But she did listen spellbound. And then Little Mary came, and it was all different. Her terrible fatigue. The impossible tasks that never ended. The cooking, shopping, all these boring chores. He never made enough money for her to have adequate help.

John's figure disappears now as darkness comes, and the click of the gate is like a shutting off of an irritating world. She is alone now, and that aloneness matters. Now the sounds come through to her, the chortling of the frogs, the slight movements of the leaves as the wind touches them. Her own tap tap of the rocker as she closes her eyes and pays attention to her thoughts and feelings now that the house and garden belong to her. She remembers herself in the mirror this very morning: blond hair, loose, even knotted; pale face, green eyes, that her father had often called the eyes of a witch, and a mouth that almost drooped though John thought her mouth her most attractive feature. He said it was a Mona Lisa mouth, mysterious, aloof, holding secrets that he knew she would never reveal. "Sometimes you're a witch," he'd say. "Sometimes you're a bitch. Sometimes you're both together, and occasionally you're simply the most alluring woman in the world." But always he would end, "Marge, why do your moods change so? Why can't you be happy for more than a few minutes at a time?" She would only smile, and he would never resent her secrecy. Open, loving John, the biologist and ecologist, who cares more about pursuing the secrets of nature than those of woman. Good in bed. Always good in bed, and he cares. Then why is she so unhappy. She never even had a career to put aside for marriage. Did she ever even have a desire for one? No, as an only child of a professor of astronomy she felt the small world around her in the university town was enough. Often as a young girl she accompanied her father during his long watches in the observatory. Because she could dream with the stars. As he watched and jotted down his notations, she considered those night splendors and made up a whole new family for herself, a family of little people whose language only she could decipher and for whom she wrote strange epic poems about giants and queens and kings and mouse people who conquered them.

Then there was no John. And then there was John. First the physical, material John, the curious, enthusiastic John, and now a John to her a kind of ghost, a shadow in the sun whose hands moved among the vegetables played over her body at night sang to Little Mary and was the quiet but beloved host at their small parties where she, holding her world shut to herself, still played the piano and sang along with the rest or dropped into her favorite rocker as she slipped away from her guests and held her own reveries with her scotch-and-soda in her hand.

The world and its people now seem to her to be eavesdroppers, listening in on her world, that is, when they turn toward her for comfort, as with Little Mary, or for companionship and sex, as with John. She knows she is living on an edge. It is not healthy to be so withdrawn from the world, even less healthy to hide from the world the fact that she is withdrawing from it. But John knows. John knows. That knowledge perhaps saves her. It makes her secret less a secret than a sharing though it isn't often she allows herself to confess this truth.

A car is inching its way up their winding driveway. That's strange. Who could it be? A colleague of John's from the lab at Woods Hole? She watches as it circles with uncertainty, stops, the driver noisily pulling up the brake. The door opens. She is not afraid. In her coolness, her aloofness, she is never afraid. She knows she has a protective cold sheeting over herself, especially over her body, that once responded so well to touch. A tall figure looks around, takes sight of her, waves, and slowly with a smile on his face approaches nearer and nearer until she knows. He is familiar all right. It is Peter. Peter Mencken, painter, husband of Carol. Peter and Carol whom they see often in the city.

"Hi, Marge," Peter says kissing her on the cheek. "Wh'cha doing sitting all alone with the stars. Eh? Where's John? I've got some good news. We took the house down the road. For a month. Carol's unpacking and Junior's pooped, ready for bed, maybe. And I'm so gosh-darned tired of driving. I had to come up here for a drink–and escape from Junior's fighting sleep. How about that drink? Eh?"

Peter is never one to let the other talk. Marge's smile of recognition is all he needs. "Get it yourself, Pete, why don't you. On the cupboard in the dining room you'll find the works."

"OK. But walk in with me, will ya? I have things to say."

"When don't you, Pete," Marge says as she eyes his peculiarly long eyelashes, his sharp nose, and boyish face. His red hair, given to Junior of course, is all fire. And his fire is contagious, she thinks with a shudder as she remembers that Christmas night when under the pretense of being too drunk to care whose bed they were in they had their once and only lovemaking together. She hadn't even felt guilty about it but she knew he did because sometimes when they happened to touch he would draw her out with his eyes and say softly, almost tearfully, "Marge, Marge." She wishes they weren't alone now. She finds two glasses and shows him where his favorite scotch is.

"But where is John?" Peter urges. "At the lab?"

"No, with the Katzes, the house to the west up the road," she says pointing. "He's having a beer. Playing poker. Not worrying, as usual."

Peter sinks into a chair in the living room. "But you're worrying as usual. Aren't you, Marge?"

She disregards his question and takes her own drink to the window seat in a darkened corner.

"Oh Christ. Come nearer, Marge. I can't see you. On the other hand, stay there. Darkness becomes you. It really does. I can barely see that mouth of yours, but I see the glint of your glass. Your lips are quite lovely sipping. You ought to *sip* more, Marge. Your sulks, you know, are quite frightening, Marge. Quite frightening."

"How's that landscape painting coming, Pete? Have you decided whether it's finished or not? You really do overdo things. You ought to stop short."

"Where? Here?" he says as he walks over to her. "God, Marge, I've missed you, really. Don't you know I'm in love with you?"

He has never said that before, not even in jest. Never even talked to her as a lover. Would he Peter Mencken be able to do what John in his casualness now never could. And what *was* that?

"Stop joking, Pete. I'm tired, really, I've cooked and sewed and cleaned. Can't think straight. Can't be social either."

"Are you ever really social, Marge? Maybe with Carol? But I mean do you give yourself at all? To anyone? Even to Little Mary? When you sing to her at night, as I know you do, is it to her you sing? Where are *you*, anyway, Marge?"

He is penetrating her for the second time, Peter, the painter-explorer. Is she pleased? He picks up her hand that lies in her lap and slowly takes it to his lips kissing it gently. She does not pull her hand away nor does she openly recognize the gesture. She keeps silent.

Pete is silent too as he lets her hand go and walks away with his drink. "I'm tired too. Damn tired. I'm leaving, Marge. Say hello to John for me, will you. See you later." She knows in his own Virginian way he means soon, tomorrow, perhaps the next day. She does not even say good-by. When she hears the door slam behind him, she takes the two glasses and walks into the kitchen with them. She puts them into the dishwasher and turns toward the stairway. She wonders why she hasn't heard the turning of the engine. No wonder, there is Peter again. In the doorway. "Forgot to kiss you good-night, Marge. Must kiss you good-night."

"No, Pete. You don't. I don't want you to." She wishes she

hadn't said anything. Resistance works less well than compliance. He'd go away then.

"But I will. I will. I want you again, Marge. I really want you, Marge."

He comes very close. "No, I'm going upstairs, Pete. To sleep."

She walks slowly up the steps. She knows he is looking at her. He does not follow.

"God, I'm tired. See you later, Marge."

Soon she hears the engine turn.

The ribbon is thin, blue. She picks it up from her bedroom floor and twirls it around her waist. It is long. Round and round she goes with the ribbon that seems endless. Where does it come from? She loosens the hold because it feels too tight, and yet she continues to make rounds and rounds of blue belting around her thin waist. It is an attractive color. Like a clear sky. Ah, she is wearing the sky around her waist. With her white blouse, she is cloud and sky. Her white cotton gauze blouse. She is diaphanous space. Her blue jeans, her blue belt, her white blouse. She is space. Air. She is air. And Peter is here. Almost next door. With his red hair. And she is air. And he is not dear John. A not-John is Peter. Does he care to wear his red hair in the air? How silly.

She walks into Little Mary's room, her blue belt trailing behind her. Mary is sleeping, on her stomach, only one side of her face visible, her hand outstretched holding Raggedy Ann, her blond hair (hair! hair!) all over the pillow. Marge walks out content. Content? Yes, content. When four-year-old Mary sleeps she makes no immediate demands.

Marge returns to the bedroom and lets the ribbon fall as she walks. She looks at the trail of sky she is leaving behind her. She'll leave the ribbon on the floor to astonish John. Will he see it? And if he does, will he think it strange or just ignore it as if whatever exists is real and therefore cannot be strange.

Marge gets to her room just as the phone rings. "Hello? This is Pete. Has John returned yet? I want to say hello to him."

"No, he's still at Lou Katz's. Why don't I tell him to see you tomorrow, Pete. It's awfully late, you know."

"Marge," he whispers. "I just wanted to hear your voice again. See you later." He hangs up. Marge slowly returns the phone to the hook.

Marge had barely gotten into bed when she hears the front door open. She hears John locking up for the night, testing windows, doors, even gas jets. Yes, dear John. Careful, fastidious, dedicated. To his family. To his plants. Should she pretend she is asleep? She listens to his footsteps on the stairway. He is at the door. He does not see the trail of blue ribbon. She watches. He looks at her and walks out again. She knows he is walking to Little Mary's room. She imagines him pulling up the covers, slightly moving Raggedy Ann away from Mary's face. He is at their door again. He walks in.

"John, is it you?"

"Oh, you're up. Good. Say, I won again. What do you think of that?"

Marge is silent.

"Kathy had hoped to come by. Too bad you wanted to be alone."

"I wasn't totally alone. Guess who's taken a house down the road."

"No good at guessing. Who?"

"Peter and Carol."

"Say that's great. How long they gonna stay?"

"A month."

"No kidding."

"Peter wanted to see you. Dead tired as he was. He really wanted to say hello. We had a drink. You'll see him tomorrow, I guess." As she talks, Marge watches John slowly take off pants, shirt, underwear, brush his teeth, look into the mirror (very slowly tonight), close the bathroom door. He is beside her now, very tender. The night passes. She is glad.

It is morning. It is night. It is morning. It is night. Today it will be different. Little Mary has already gleefully escaped with the blue ribbon. Little Mary has left with John. Early. She is to be with him all day at the lab. John will drop by the Menckens' before they leave. Peter will have his hello in his rented house. Marge hopes her rented house will be just hers all day. She won't do a single chore. First, she'll practice the piano. Then take a long walk in her special part of the Cape, away from west and east and south, where all the people are, then have a quiet lunch. Read Christina Snead's *The Man Who Loved Children*. Even take a nap. Have her tea alone. Then of course at five she will have to prepare dinner. Never complete freedom, after all.

Never a plan carried out either, she realizes as she hears a knock at the door. Oh no, Pete again. "Didn't John and Little Mary say hello to you this morning, Pete?"

"Yes, but I want to continue our conversation of last night."

"Oh, Pete. What conversation?"

"About you. About us. Everything I said I meant, you know, Marge. I simply have to see you. To be with you. Completely."

She wants air. She wants space. Peter is here, with his red hair. Marge walks into the garden. Pete follows. She is on the hammock rocking. She smiles.

"You're sulking, Marge. You're not listening. Not caring. Don't you care?"

She wants air. She wants space. Pete is here, with his red hair. "How is Carol, Pete? And Junior?"

"You don't want to be disloyal to Carol, is that it, Marge? She really doesn't mind what I do, you know. Now that she's into the new novel. She really doesn't care, you know."

"I care."

"For John? For Carol? Or for me, Marge?"

"For me, Pete. For me." Pete is here, with his red hair. He is fumbling with a stick. He pokes it into the sand. The sand shimmers, like Pete's hair. She is the sand. How many specks of sand is she. How many. Peter is stepping on her. He is walking to the hammock. He is sitting beside her. He is holding her hand. He is kissing her. She is sinking into his arms. He is whispering. He is holding her tightly, tightly. They are in the bedroom. They are frantic. Clothes are helter-skelter. She is moaning. A terrible rocking. Now they are cool. Subdued. "Pete," she is saying. "Go home. Go home."

It is morning. It is night. She has taken up knitting. The stitches are falling. She is knitting a sweater for Little Mary. She may do one for John, for his thirty-fifth birthday. They will celebrate it in the city. With Pete and Carol, of course. Pete is painting her portrait. She does not like it. He is better with landscapes. No figures. Figures threaten him. Last year his painting of the sand won him a Childe Hassam. He will not win a prize for his portraits. He is all fire. Fire on the sand.

Bellows

IT WAS on the wall standing upright–not a hanging piece nor a relief. It was simply leaning. As if for some support. To her it was hardly a work of art, and its simple lines and rugged exterior, made of plaster of Paris still hardening, with its overall whiteness, made it stark and ominous. She could hardly tell its shape. Long, lean, with protruding center an oval shape, it seemed more a once-functional gigantic bellows than a work of art. But James said it was a work of art when he brought her here the first time. Told her not to touch it. That it was fragile. Needed repair. He was going to repair it before finally allowing her to keep it as a memento of their relationship. But he had never done a thing to it. Nor to their relationship for that matter. Their relationship was as still and functional in its quiet way as the so-called work of art. It was always the same–stark, standing still, yet foreboding. Of what she cared not to think. Of course what could it be looking toward? A split. A breakup. That was always momentary. Rather immediate. Perhaps on the way, yet immediate. Each time it was good-by. Yet the hello was more in her remembrance than the good-by. Because there was always the hello. Four months. Twice a week. Hello good-by hello good-by. This token. This little leaning tower reminding her of fragility, of the fragility of their affair.

She walked over to the window and looked out. The room was barren except for a single three-quarter bed and a white dresser with three drawers (one of which she could not open), on the top of which stood a lonely phone, and the awkward bellows of course against the wall. This room was not a place to live in. It too was purely functional. But was a room where love took place functional? Rather obscene that. Love after all was larger, more expansive. Maybe it made the "work" bellow out, open and close to let air in, the world. Maybe that was why that ominous white thing remained against the wall. To allow a possibility of breathing, of opening out to something other than a bed and a chest of drawers (with that unworkable drawer). But when James gave her that present as a reminder of something to come, an ending to come, he hardly thought of it as symbolic she was sure. He never thought in symbols. His world was *functional*. Here was a room in lower Manhattan, a kind of pied-à-terre, where love could take place unhindered and yet where there would be both a reminder of his career (going terribly well, she thought bitterly as she ached to think of her last manuscript return) and a reminder that even this relationship would end, immediately, presently, momentarily. There it was, the still drying plaster of Paris leaning against a wall, threatening, yet giving assurance of something concrete, an end. Ends were to James more important than beginnings. Though his hello was ever so sweet, and his good-by rather gruff and unendurable.

She looked out of the window for some talisman. All she could see were the tops of buildings. Their room was on the fourteenth floor in an apartment of Washington Square Village. All around were old, dingy apartment houses, mostly in the process of being torn down or of being remodeled for more expensive residences. She thought of the area in Paris near the Beaubourg where old, cheap buildings were being remodeled into unattractive rich apartments so the very rich could have a place to call their own in the oldest district in Paris. She knew the displaced poor were more displaced than ever. Always giving up a small piece of dwelling, old, beaten down, to move on to even smaller places more beaten down, more unlivable. And the rich, marauders ever, were demolishing, destroying, making the old new, livable. Yet, she knew, unbearable. How were the poor to live when the rich encroached upon them. She recalled the mayor's recent remark that either one earned $40,000 a year or nothing if one wished to live in New York. It wasn't her $40,000 that kept her here. It was James's. His need for her. Momentarily. His encroachment upon her. Her willingness to subsist. Her ache, her longing.

She turned from the barren window view to the room. She looked at the dresser on which the white phone seemed less contact than withdrawal from a world. A tiny phone. Nothing on the dresser other than it. Her own small toilet things were placed neatly in the first drawer; the second only other workable drawer contained extra underthings for both of them – his light robe too, swimming trunks, and three extra towels. It was his idea always to have three extra towels. She never did understand the number three. Not four? Was it hers that was the one not added? She the diminished one? The one not needing anything extra, not even an extra towel?

She sat on the edge of the bed, near the phone. Should she call him? Give his secretary their code. "This is Ms. Moffett calling, of the Rudford Gallery. Do tell Mr. Shelton that the wood he ordered has arrived. It will be available for pickup at five-thirty today." He would then call or come by at five-thirty. That he did do. Promptly at five-thirty something would happen. Messages to him were always delivered, and he carried out their instructions. Always. A little too quickly. Almost without imagination. He was a disciplined person. An artist who worked hard, expected her to work hard too. And to play. Regularly. With discipline. No ragged edges: that is, without requests, demands, sighs, hopes, new kinds of meetings, travel plans, etc. No, she was to meet him in this room twice a week. And it would be complete. Feverish, fun, feisty, with the imminent farewell – that is, merely a good-by or the inevitable: that finale, that final good-by. Without remorse. Without tears. Without regrets.

It was as if he were measuring a piece of wood for one of his constructions. Everything was orderly. Functional. She was part of his world of elegant functioning. So far she had played that game – and well. At any rate, she would continue to do so. At least today. She picked up the phone and delivered her message. It was five o'clock. She would have half an hour to wait. She opened her bag and took out her notebook. She read from her new manuscript the poem she was working on. What troubled her in it was the word *functional.* Was the "k" sound too cacophonous? She tried other words: *useful, utilitarian, workable, quotidian, maneuverable, working, easeful, satisfactory.* No no no. She would have to allow the cacophony.

There was the sound of a key turning in the door. She looked at her watch: it was five-thirty.

Stars, Etc.

WE LIE side by side, having just made love. Even as I lie near you, not looking at you, but touching, I see your eyes. They still have the stars of love. When speaking of love there is nothing that is more true than the cliché–the lover must not avoid such words as *stars* (see above), or moon, or sun, or coral lips, or the rose. The lover who makes love has been fearless and bold in his love maneuvers. No parts of the body have been ignored. So must the lover be bold in his use of language: above all, he must use the cliché. *Your eyes are like stars; your lips are like coral; you are the moon, the sun. I love you. Do you love me,* etc.

So I think of the stars in your eyes as I lie beside you. You are speaking, but I only hear the music of your voice. The words never reach my ears. My ears are the funnels through which love passes. Your music plays inside me anyway (my body is the silent harp being played upon–again, no avoidance of the cliché, *see above*). I know when you touch me you are touching silk, cool silk (you have just noted that ten minutes ago), and when I touch you I am touching fire (I have just noted that ten minutes ago), and so as you speak your words come to me as music. I am smiling. Only occasionally do I say "oh" or "really?" Your sweet monologue is now my harp. You do not notice that my responses are monosyllables. Monologue, monosyllables. We are good together, ah good together, even when lying still, merely touching.

I am sure many minutes go by in this fashion. Maybe even an

hour. And it is like a pattern of time because of course soon we are touching fearlessly again (*see above*) and so after more time, close time, we return to the original position described above merely touching I hearing your words of music, then I becoming the harp, I saying *oh really,* you telling something a story perhaps as the words funnel through my ears, music to me, music passing through my ears. And do I say that stars are in your eyes (probably in mine too but I cannot see me and you not being one to use language as if you are a poet never say you see stars in my ears. I don't recall your describing my eyes at all in fact. Do you?) I probably do not say that–you would feel embarrassed to hear me say that time and time again. It is not your style to listen to such language–too often. Oh yes you like to hear it once. Sometimes I wish you would like to hear it more often because when I am in love it is difficult for me to use new words. *See above.* There we are, languishing (*see above*).

We know that soon we will have to occupy ourselves with the business at hand. The business at hand whatever it is we know is not love. It is going to an office, a lab, the market (that is, the food market, or even, if the style of life makes one so inclined, the stock market). The business at hand is simply always at hand.

It is ridiculous to turn from hands of love to the business at hand. It is always difficult to make that shift but the surprising thing is that once having made that shift no one not even ourselves sees anything peculiar in the act. We go about our business in shirt or dress, pants or skirt without any trace in our behavior of what has just passed between us. We use other clichés. No more in our language the clichés of love but the clichés of work. The passing of the day, even the good-mornings, hellos, the questions, the curt or other replies to important practical matters never seem inconsistent with what has just transpired. Having been transformed our transcendence becomes unremarkable unremarked upon. Strange business this passing of the day passing from love to the market (metaphor here, please note).

So it is that this particular day is not a particular day. You have lain beside me I beside you. We have seen stars. Or rather I have seen stars in your eyes and of course you have seen stars (or at least I can call them so when I remember the shock, the physical shocks those stars become as you lie beside me and I have felt those shocks in me, etc.) We have gotten up and have had our–is it breakfast, brunch, lunch? No, not lunch or dinner because we both have to proceed to the market (metaphor, *see above*). As we kiss good-by, you going your way, me mine, it becomes an ordinary day. I dress, put on the usual makeup (we have showered of course this day, as I remember, not together–therefore, it must be an ordinary day, a weekday). We probably have appointments. Maybe it is you who have the appointment or I, I do not now remember. Anyway we miss that particular special event, that showering together, but it does not seem so crucial and it would have been too excruciating, the pleasure, that is, so that the appointments would not have been met on time and perhaps the stars would have lingered to interfere with the ordinariness of the appointment, the market would have been a bit defiled or perhaps corrupted or perhaps even blessed, too blessed in the usual sense and the market never has that particular blessing. The ordinariness is never tainted with the residues of bed (the office maneuvers or sexual innuendoes notwithstanding). At any rate, we are both not together. You have gone your way I mine. I wish I can remember who has the appointment. However, it really doesn't matter, does it. Because our demeanor, should I say demeanors, is there such a word–our demeanors are not remarkable that day. We are now using language of the market *(see above)*, the clichés of the market. We ignore the fact that it is only the clichés of love one knows for sure, all other language is evasive, unreal, ambiguous–there is no telling what one means.

We both go our way. Neither of us knowing what we mean as we talk seriously to this or that person, make this or that computation on paper, on typewriter, in lab, in radio station, in interview, in office. We are not even noticing that time is being consumed, that the day will end, that our lunch appointments, dinner appointments, telephone calls, so busily enacted, so scrupulously attended are marking time, enabling us to get our checks so that we can go on to meeting ourselves at some appointed hour. We only know that our attention to the market (*see above*) is a kind of enabling act that allows us to proceed from that market to ourselves so that we can each in his/her respective way feel the stars in our eyes, etc.

It is not you who are saying all these things. You are always one to consider the office, the lab, the radio station, etc. to be important. You will not concede that the funnel through which your words to me become music is the important communicant. No, you will not make that concession. Your actions belie your thoughts. You are most yourself–in bed you never ask *who am I?*–when you lie beside me. That I am most myself then we need not even question. No quibbling there. And make no sexual connection either. Neither of us pretends otherwise. Our identities are never more firm, more realistic than when we are together being ourselves, each the other, each the one, very firmly the one–or the togetherness would never have happened. Once you had even accepted that verbally. You said, do you remember, *the body never lies*. I could interpret your statement as I wished. I think I said: *What does the body say?* We had different interpretations to that one, but it never seemed to matter. It confirmed everything that needed confirmation and we were both happy.

Happiness. To get to that. Do we try to understand that day or any previous day? Or do we just accept happiness as being with each other, I lying next to you, you next to me, and the nonquestions that become music in my ears and wherever the music goes to you. You said once my body was cool. Maybe music from me to you lies in the coolness of my body or the fire in yours that the coolness in mine evokes.

Happiness. Why don't we skip that thought. And just accept it as a fact. The stars in your eyes, etc. *See above*.

To return to the day at hand. At hand! Hands are always so important in this love business. In this life business. The meeting that takes place in the Madison Avenue office. We must get to the business at hand. Perhaps you are sitting at the head of the conference table. Your secretary is taking notes. You are wearing a tie. Your pants are sparklingly pressed. Your eyes, those blue eyes, suggest nothing but the business at hand. Mr. X and Mr. Y are presenting reports. You are listening. You do not even nod your head. "Has anyone anything to add?" you ask. Only Mr. B wants to add something, but he is afraid. You know he is afraid because of the way he stirs in his chair. You look at him. Once. You do not want to press him. He turns away. "If there is nothing to add," you say, "we shall have the report typed. You will all proceed accordingly."

You have turned from the bed to the cab to the office. You have listened to the report. You are firm, solid, stolid. You have acted in the market. *See above.*

I have already prepared my talk. I have taken a cab, have made inquiries of my secretary. Have received the person at the appointed hour. (We both that day have had appointments?) I am wearing a black wool poplin skirt, a high-buttoned white silk blouse, an alpaca and wool sweater-jacket with gigot sleeves and shaped waist, on which is a small antique pin (I had bought it in Geneva five years ago). It has just a mite of coral so that its elegance is clear even to the stranger with whom I have an appointment. I am saying: *I don't understand the plot. Your novel seems confused. Yes of course I understand you want a structure that holds the ambiguities of life itself. But you understand Mr. K the market today [see above] cannot take ambiguities. They are simply not commercial. Are you a literary writer?* I stare at him. This accusation unnerves him. He is beginning to stutter. I am undaunted. "You see, as I read your novel, I do not find any sex. Don't you see that this is an egregious omission?"

Of course I do not relate that question to my morning episodes. I hear no music whatsoever in my ears or anywhere as I make these remarks. "There is no sex," he is saying, "but there is violence. Violence is better than sex. It oversexes sex," he is adding. "It exceeds in shock and sensation sex itself."

I am listening. He is saying, "There is a drowning of a baby, an axing of a wife, a shooting of a ten-year-old boy whose body is cut up, mangled in a meat grinder, and then disposed of in a safe deposit box in the East River near Sixty-eighth Street. What about that?"

"Come, Mr. K," I say undaunted. "All that is old hat. Have you no new kinds of violence? Anyway, I hate to say this, Mr. K, but your style is too romantic. It needs to be more suggestive. Too many clichés."

I ignore my firm belief in the clichés of love. (*See above.*)

"I regret I must return your manuscript. I am sure some other publisher will be happy to publish the work. I'm afraid it isn't for us. It has been a pleasure to meet you, Mr. K. Good-by." I extend my hand and smile.

I do not watch Mr. K leave the office. The telephone is ringing. I am beginning to think of my evening talk as I prepare for lunch at the Algonquin with an author who has just the right mixture of sex and violence. I am about to ask my secretary to hand me the manuscript of the author with whom I am having lunch when the phone rings again and it is you.

You say *hello*. My body begins to sing. I am hearing music in my ears, desire is creeping along its usual ways and I am saying *oh really*. The monosyllables the monologue are on. But you are asking to see me right away. For lunch. You have just had to accept an appointment in Nebraska for tomorrow. You cannot see me tonight. But you want to talk today. *Oh,* I say. *Yes,* I say. I cancel my appointment at the Algonquin. I meet you within the hour in the French restaurant in the Fifties we like so much. We are holding each other's hands. There is no business at hand. *See above*. I am not thinking of the talk I have already prepared for the evening. You are not thinking of the Nebraska appointment. There are stars in your eyes. I know there must be stars in mine. "You have stars in your eyes," I say. *See above*.

Virginia Farm

IT IS two o'clock in the afternoon and the cat is dead. The boys are out on the lawn playing Frisbee. The mother with soiled apron is churning the butter in the newly purchased electric churn. As luck would have it, the churn doesn't work. Hands would be better, but churning with hands hurts. She lets the unmade butter, liquefied, slightly churned, stand, with the top of the machine steeped in electric innards, uncapped. She places the churn on the table and turns to the dishes of the morning. The dishwasher broke a month ago. There are many dishes. The plumber had oiled the thing insisting that oil was all it needed. It needs more. What more, she does not know.

She begins washing the cups of the morning, of five mornings and five evenings. The boys are arguing about their game. She knows they do not know about the cat. Secretly she wishes they did. They would bury it, and Tom would cry. He would have nightmares. She would soothe him. He would rest in her arms. He would fall asleep. She would kiss him on the forehead. He would sleep peacefully. But Steve would not have nightmares. He would delight in the burial. He would make it a whole-day affair. He would make a small casket. It would take him hours and hours to find the precise kind of wood. He would steal the nails from the shed that his father prohibited him from ever using. He would take the hammer and would hurt his thumb. He always hurt his thumb. He would crush it. It would bleed. He'd relish that. He would let the blood remain on the wood. His signature. His casket. Four hours later he would seek the proper burial spot.

Tom's face would be streaked with dirt from his tears. His despair. He would stoop. Horror would give him the chills. Steve would direct Tom: *Do this, do that. Find a white sheet. A large needle. Sew our shroud.*

Steve would make up his mumbo-jumbo, his prayer. His last sacrament. *Rest, cat, in thy bower. Grace to thy bones and eternal heat to you.*

No, Tom would say, *not "heat." Shut up,* Steve would shout. *Eternal heat to you in heavenly hell. Amen.*

Say, Amen, he would command Tom. *Say Amen.*

Tom would say *Amen* and run. Run to his bed. His nightmare. She would come at night prowling like the cat smothering Tom with her love. He in her arms. Steve would have found a shovel that day, would pile the heaps of sand onto the cat grave. He would sing a heavenly hymn to Satan, his lord. Oh my god, she thinks, washing her fifteenth cup, it is two o'clock in the afternoon and the cat is dead.

Black Snake

At first he thinks it is a black feather or a limp balloon or the tail of a bird. He ignores it, gets on with his shaving when he sees the thing jerk. He walks up to it, sees that though the thing seems to dangle before his window screen what is before him is only part of the thing, part of a long swooping tubular living object. He turns his head upward to look at this strange extension. Resting almost perpendicular before him on the shingles of his rented cottage is a large snake with a foreboding bulge–this is no picture-book snake. It is real and the thing has gorged a mouse. He is watching a primitive act of digestion.

To calm himself he returns to his bathroom mirror and tries to continue shaving. He notices the shaking of his hand. He holds his razor taut testing his poise. It takes a while for him to hold the razor firmly enough not to cut his face. He dares not look out the window. Should he try to kill the snake? Get a broom? A pole? Or the caretaker, even the sheriff if there is such a person? In New York at least he'd call the police and they'd come tearing up the street, their sirens shrieking–prepared with hoses axes picks and god knows what new apparatus. But to kill a snake? Will a broom do? And what if it isn't poisonous? Why kill a living creature just because your guts are falling out of fear. Primeval, or is it city fear? My god, he was quaking, afraid to remain in the cottage. He'd never go to bed! Snakes in bed. He may as well be an old maid waiting for the phallus–the man under the bed, the snake in the window. He finishes his shaving. But he can't resist walking up to the window again, studying the long black ominous form with the obscene bulge. Of course the bulge is a mouse. Maybe even a rat. Or don't snakes eat rats. He walks more cautiously but the monster is still there. He feels sick to his stomach.

He'll have to tell the caretaker about the serpent in his garden. Bill walks to the main house. The caretaker smirks with unconcealed country glee, says he'll get rid of the snake that morning. He assures Bill it isn't poisonous. He's a good snake, he says. He'll clean out the hay in the barn. I'll take care of *him,* he says, with a twinkle that is a country putdown of snake-fearing, city slicker Bill Hamilton.

Bill feels like a child reprimanded by his mother for eating the last sliver of pie she was saving for his dad. He is angry. He is thirty-six years old, with three novels behind him. He is a man all right. Has even been in the ring. Professional. In Dallas. As he walks back to the cottage, he knows he's stooping, like a big forlorn bear. He is wearing his long-sleeved tan wool sweater over a white shirt. He knows he's ludicrous. Too god-damn clean. Too well shaven. A stooping six-footer with broad shoulders and a fear of a perfectly good, perfectly reasonable creature trying to help our ecological dung. Would clean out the hay. Would enable cows, horses, god knows who, to eat a good hearty hay breakfast. He is a little boy. A spoiled brat. A mommy's boy who even took dancing lessons when he was ten.

He is hungry. He'll take the car and eat in a diner. Wherever he can find one. He remembers a string of ugly motels the night he rented the cottage. Probably a diner in one of them. He throws his body into the front seat, puts the key in the ignition. It won't start. Angry, he tries again and again. He places his foot firmly on the gas. Holds it there while he turns the key. The engine turns over. With a jolt the car moves. He drives down the long dirt road of the farm, passing the neat rows of boxwood, and turns right. He drives at least ten miles before he sees any signs of life. Motels suddenly appear in their brutal plainness giving the Virginia countryside a drabness that used to be the sign of only eastern or midwestern city limits. Here are buildings built only to satisfy bare and elementary needs of a traveler: bed and board. He is running away from a snake only to get into America's snakepit. He remembers the area where he had driven in at night. Low yellow lights ensnaring the tired visitor. Food, drink, probably sex as well. Yet a couple of shots of whiskey can make one forget the sagging face in the mirror behind the bartender. A twentieth-century oval with holes for eyes and a mouth that has downed whiskey, swallowed valium.

Bill drives into a roadway with only three parked cars. He turns off his ignition. Shutting the door behind him he walks slowly to the diner, determined not to drink at least until after breakfast.

He orders ham and eggs and looks around at the desolate tables. There is only a haggard-looking girl at the far end of the diner. She doesn't interest him. When he left Katie for his Virginia trip, he promised himself he would remain uninvolved. Lovely Katie, with her wild eyes, her mad dreams. She has given him enough of women for the year. Good in bed, she allows him his freedom, doesn't care a damn for his writing, never interferes with his working hours, has the sense to leave him alone with his beers and buddies at the frequent times when beer means more to him than a bed. Yet she is a singing bird: sweet, a real sport, and he has to admit terribly intelligent. They never "talk," she's too aloof for the grand discussion or too frightened of her own existential terrors to get too serious with him or anyone else. A tenderness comes over him as he remembers her funny disguises. She's a whirling Isadora Duncan in a wisp of a Pucci gown or she's a child reciting a brutal nightmare as if it were "Old Ironsides." He frowns as he tries to forget her last dream. "I was on a rice paddy in Vietnam when the war stopped, and *I* stopped. A corpse. I saw an angel on the thumb of a dead baby. I went up to it, plucked its wings and flew right into your arms. You fucked me. I cried because you gave me back the dead baby." In some way he really did. That's one reason, he thinks, he took this trip.

"Coffee, sir?"

"Yes, black." He is hungry he realizes as he picks up the cup. He remembers the black snake. The devil, he thinks, and smiles as he congratulates himself on his unconscious pun. A tap on his arm makes him look up. It is the haggard girl. He hadn't even heard her come up to him.

"Listen, take me with you. I'm desperate. Just left a good friend on the road. He dropped me off. Take me with you. What do you say?"

First a black snake, then an unhappy girl. He is beginning to believe in omens.

"Take me with you," she repeats as he eyes her cagily.

"Look, I'm a stranger. Maybe a notorious rapist sought by the FBI. I'm an awful bad guy," he says unconvincingly. "But talk, go ahead. Talk. I'm a good listener besides being a rapist."

"I don't talk. Take me with you." Her empty eyes plead with him.

He feels nothing. She is stone. Amorphous. All he wants is for her to go away. She's not even flesh. No body. Emaciated. A thing. A mouse. Like that bulge in the snake. She's been devoured. He is seeing the mouse. "Have you ever seen a black snake," he asks crazily.

"Yes. Back the road a bit. We thought we'd stop off at a farmhouse to rent a cottage. And we saw this long black thing hanging straight down a shingle. It was be–yoo–tiful." For the first time she smiles.

"That's my snake," he says, and he is sorry. Now she knows he has a place to stay.

"Oh, take me to him. I love snakes. I'll train him for you. Please," and her empty eyes light up from some place deep within her.

"No, it's no longer my place," he lies. "I left it this morning. And I hate snakes. Listen, I'm hungry. Do you mind," and he begins to eat.

"I'll share your ham and eggs," she is saying.

"I'll order some for you. Waitress," he says as the waitress turns her head, "another order of ham and eggs."

"And toast and coffee," the girl adds.

She knows what she wants, he thinks, handling his knife and fork slowly, deliberately, as if he is playing chess.

She stares in front of her lost in her empty eyes. When her order comes, she eats quickly as if she hasn't eaten for days. "Could I have more toast," she asks Bill with tears in those eyes.

"Of course," he says signaling to the waitress, giving the new order.

"Toast is good, isn't it," she says, "when you're hungry."

"Yes, toast is good," What will he do with the girl. She's a clinger, a leech. No wonder the guy left her on the road. Probably had all he could bear. Picked her up, had her, dropped her. She looks as if she's seen plenty. Why did she have to find *him*?

"Listen, mind my coffee, will you. I'm going to the bathroom."

Mind her coffee. What a strange idea. Like a schoolgirl in a dining hall. Mind her coffee. Should I run now. Should I pay and run. Why not, he thinks, as he drinks the last drop of his coffee. But he wants more coffee. No sooner thought than poured. Some waitresses are uncanny. He looks at this one—about fifty-five, neat, troubled. Lines under her eyes, her coiffure (a wig?) magically tidy, and hands red with too much dishwashing. She does have a lovely voice.

"Anything else, sir?"

"Were you ever a singer," he asks.

"How did you know?" Her eyes are not dead. Rather lovely, misty, alive.

"Where?"

"You wouldn't believe it. In the Blue Cafe."

"Really?" he says pretending to know the place. Probably a celebrated nightspot nearby.

"But I won't tell you how many years ago."

"I bet I know. Four?"

"Oh, you're a gentleman," she says and laughs as she turns away.

The girl is coming back. He watches her slow steps and thinks he notices a limp. It seems like something new. "Say, you're limping. Did you hurt yourself?"

"No, I'm a victim. Of polio."

I'm a victim. Of polio. She puts things oddly. She sits, dropping her hands lifeless on the counter.

"I'm sorry. Look here, though. I can't take you. I've got to go. But why don't I leave you something. You know, for eating breakfast with me. As a kind of thanks. OK?" He says as he places under her limp hand a ten-dollar bill. Tears stream down her cheeks. She does not even say thank-you as she clutches the bill. He gets up. She does not ask him to stay. She has only wanted money! For the second time that morning he feels sick to his stomach.

Cosmetic Instrument

SHE IS STANDING far away from the spot on the couch where the wine had spilled. The red wine, a weak Beaujolais. On the white couch. She is standing in the far corner of the long living room. She is standing far away from that corner couch. She is looking at that couch. Will she get rid of it because of that single deep red spot? Because of the spot? Or because of the history of the spot?

She is not looking at the spot now. She is sitting. Sitting at her desk in the upstairs bedroom. She is alone. She is holding a pen. She is asking for forgiveness. She is writing a letter to Ralph asking for forgiveness. *It is not because I do not love you. It was all impulse. All impulse. Why did I take the scissors, a gift from John from Switzerland. Why did I take the scissors and on an impulse grab your hand and stab that hand, that hand that had been an instrument of your love? It was an impulse. Yes, an impulse. And after all the wound was slight. Only the blood flowed. But not flowed. No, oozed. I see you running to the bathroom faucet. Pouring peroxide on that wound. I see the white foam. I hear the hissing. I see your pale face. I see the hatred in your face. I am caught in the net of that hatred now. And I now know that hatred is as near love as blood is near the surface of the skin. Don't you know that too?*

She has written it all down. She has put down matter-of-factly that she was ready to kill. That her intentions were murderous. She was not pouting, not being coy or merely uncivil. She had made a gesture of murder. She had been violent. Impulsive, unrestrained, irrational. And unmotivated. What had Ralph done? He had been sitting next to her, holding his wine glass in one hand and her own hand in the other. He had dropped her hand in order to light a cigarette. Had squeezed it ever so gently before making the move toward the lighter. In that instant, she had grabbed the scissors lying so casually on the cocktail table. (How inelegant could she be, a scissors on her table before the arrival of Ralph? A murderous intent, a premeditated act?) She had grabbed the scissors and had quickly taken his hand, turned it over so that the palm was available, available for that dagger thrust. Her movements were so quick Ralph was absolutely stunned as he watched not her but the red wine oozing onto the couch. She was so quick she too was stunned as she watched the blood ooze. In a moment she had become an expert in violence: she had the speed, the maneuverability, the weapon. She had it all there before the act. After such knowledge, what forgiveness? She could not forgive herself. The knowledge was the act. The act followed the impulse. The cause of the impulse remained even now unknown.

It was John she hated, not Ralph. It was John she wished to hurt. Manipulation of memory, reversal of intent. Substitution of lovers. Sublimation of feeling. Responsiveness to stimulus. Responsiveness to past hurt. Activity processed out of mind, no, out of hand through feeling. What gut told what story of what passion. What passion led to what sequence of events. Event is hard fact. The process of it, that is, the sequence of feelings toward the fact, still unknown. Better unknown. She would not try to probe for reasons. The irrational is superior to the rational. Instinct is authenticity. Reason is manipulative; therefore, not authentic. She is looking for authenticity. In act, in heart. She sits at her desk, puts down her pen. She looks out of the window. At the broken fence covering the hydrangea bush, damaging the hydrangea bush. The fence is made of old wood, of the birch tree the hurricane had toppled, the birch that had been shaped into thin poles flattened and then rounded at the ends. She watches a squirrel run up and down the poles. Another smaller squirrel follows. They are playing some kind of tag. They leave the fence and run up the bare-limbed branches of the dogwood tree. How quickly they scramble from branch to branch. Lithe creatures. Not loathing. Playing. They negotiate each branch as if it were as thick and wide as a tiled roof. Without fear. Dexterity. Unconcern with the spaces all around them. If one should fall, what would the other do? Run away? Come to its aid, drag it to a squirrel home? Under, in what tree do these particular squirrels live? Are these squirrels *chez moi?* How do I give them stability, sanctity, the right not to be considered trespassers?

She turns away from the window. Goes down to the living room. Opens the drawer of the antique desk that John had given her only two years ago for her birthday and takes out the scissors. She had cleaned it thoroughly. Not a trace of blood. Who could tell what treacherous act it had committed? Could detectives discover her bestiality? But Ralph would keep it all to himself out of shame. So slight a matter, only a matter between the two of them. A matter that separated skin from blood vessel, that separated Ann Beaton from Ralph Lenz. A simple matter after all. It told only the story of her life, but even as it told it, it concealed it. The act had been direct, immediate, without digression. The reason for it still smothered in blood vessels that were where–in the head or the heart or the arms? Who had asked her recently where she considered her unconscious to be? Oh yes, a poet. He did not like her answer: that it was everywhere. He thought another poet had a much more suggestive response: in the throat, he had said. In the throat. Was that really so preposterous a reply as she had thought at the time? Or was hers, that it was everywhere, a more ridiculous retort. She knew she had said that out of total repression because she really thought her unconscious was in her head. Where she considered all memory, all thought lay. Was she not right? The unconscious even as it gathered up the instinctual, the irrational, the archetypal, certainly could not gather itself into some kind of laryngeal refuge. *But she has glottal stop.* Oh no. Punning won't relieve her, won't solve the problem of her violence. Is she then, has she always been potentially violent? One action is never complete in itself. It must go backward and forward. Out of the deep past into a present, and protruding into a future. Of course she could go to her old analyst. But he never had helped her. And how does she know that help is what she now needs? Maybe it is not Ralph, not John, but all men. Maybe this is the result of her sympathy for the women's movement. It led to spontaneous eruptions of overt acts of hostility toward men, any man, lover, husband, friend. And though Ralph was a lover whom she trembled, ached in her love to be with, she obviously felt him a proper target of woman's cumulative hate. She had thrust her manicuring scissors into his palm. She had committed an act of hate toward a man she thought she loved. And what did he do? Run to the faucet, clean the wound, pour peroxide over it, place a Band-Aid on the now dry cut, stride out of the bathroom, hall, living room, walk to the closet, take one look at her through the hall mirror, gaze for a moment at his own pale face, adjust the Band-Aid, open the door, walk out. She had never said a single word. Nor had he. After two years, he had simply walked out of her door. After two years, she had simply cut the hand that fed her her existence, her hope, her heart. For two years he had made existence possible, even a future possible, as it had been with John before their divorce. Time was no longer dreary. She had found that her one single self could multiply–not through a child, she had never wanted children–but through her lover. One and another. A lover made two in one. Such arithmetic was begotten out of tenderness. Recently invitations always ended with, "And do invite handsome Ralph." The simplicity of the thing, before. Now silence. Now guilt. Not a guilt of deception as their first year of love had been before her divorce but a guilt of murderous intent. Of a horrendous deed committed, not even long premeditated. A deed spontaneous and terrible. She holds the scissors in her hands as if it were a talisman, a tender offering from god, a gift from a beloved (as indeed it had been). Yes, it is a gift from a beloved. It showed her the complexity of love. It showed her that a love thrust could be as dire as rape. The love act, it told her, was not a simple motion growing out of a growing fever, a yearning for physical release. The love act could tear the flesh, pierce even an open palm. She looks yearningly at the scissors. Tears fall from her eyes. This little weapon, this cosmetic aid, she had propelled into her lover's palm. It was then an instrument of love! And yes an instrument of hate. Therefore, it held in itself a complex of emotions, a true love since love was so complex, since love contained the ambiguity of hate and love, since its duplicity was not a duplicity of evil, but a container of the double vision of love itself: the love that looked inward and saw in the love act the symbol of those tensions within it, that simple ambiguity of love: the motions of love that propelled relief and joy also moved in a manner of force, of powerful thrust so that pain could be its accompaniment. Was not that frictional thrust a thrust of hate as well as of love? Was not the physical embodiment the dialectic of love? Her act of violence was thus a symbolic act of love. The pain she inflicted was her love. It was an erotic maneuver. It was physical love.

She walks over to the window holding the scissors in her right hand. The sun is casting shadows, shadows of trees on the roof of the house opposite to her. The shadows are absolutely motionless. She holds up the scissors toward the sun. The points gleam. Sparkle. She moves the prongs nearer to the window. They glint and seem to make her hand warm. She makes small circles with the scissors on the cold window. Now the glint is in her eyes. She feels its penetration. That glint is not circumspect. Not hidden. It is making her smile. She opens her mouth and begins to hum. It is Beethoven's *Ode to Joy*. Over and over again she hums the initial phrase, never able to reach the final tonic note. She hums, and hums. Suddenly she stops. The room is filled with her laughter. She laughs and laughs and laughs. The scissors fall out of her hand. Tears begin to flow. She cannot stop those tears. Her whole body is crying. She is on the floor. *I am guilty,* she is whispering between the sobs. An hour passes. She lies quietly, still on the floor. Her eyes open. She hears herself saying over and over, *I am guilty. I am guilty.* She is frowning, frowning. She is puzzled. *Of what am I guilty?* she asks.

Eloquence

I WON'T HEAR OF IT," she said as she closed the large doors behind her. He remained in the room staring into space. It was at least a thirty-foot living room, with a large grand piano, a circular couch (a rather dirty gold), an octagonal low-sitting cocktail table, and an occasional upholstered chair barely filling up the spaces. Paintings of the kind that filled Victorian houses hung gloomily on the walls: portraits with antiqued gold frames, two or three watercolors, an eccentrically stylized still life, a gouache landscape of a rather subtle blue (the only subtlety in the room) with what was either a vulture or a raven depicted in the upper right-hand corner. Also a rather "pretty" Manguin. Nothing at all particularly noteworthy hung on those high-ceilinged walls.

As one entered, to the left there was an old grandfather clock that actually worked. The chimes were rather ghastly on the quarter hour. Lucy said you got used to that, he remembered. Her father had bought it in Switzerland over fifty years ago at a time when anything Swiss seemed beautiful to him. It was because of the girl, her mother. Coming from an old Genevan family, she had the cold bearing that always entices the exuberant American. She was married at the time, to the son of an old watchmaking millionaire. She even had a child. Lucy came as the result of a swift affair, carried on, as her father always related, with about the same passion (on her part) as the eating of a fondue dinner. Her taste was for American men. Her husband was debonair about it all. A man twenty years older than his wife, he indulged in good wines, business deals, chamber music, and superbly tailored suits. It was only in his ties that one saw a bit of indecision, Lucy's father said–a secret despair that finally led to his suicide at the age of forty-eight. Strangely enough, after that, the wife cut off all affairs. Her life became resolute, virginal. She took to business deals. Rather odd for a Swiss woman at the time. And she never had anything more to do with Lucy or her father. Lucy was brought up by an American aunt, in New York. Governesses, good schools, a year in Florence, another year of art in New York, and marriage. Two children, and one affair. His.

But this time it was really coming to a head. He was sick of meeting at the Pierre, the carefully arranged room for the night, the quick departure after breakfast. After five years of this sort of thing, he had insisted on coming to her house. Aghast at first at his visit, she talked coolly about the possibility of her getting a divorce. Just five minutes before she had agreed, rather sweetly in fact, and then abruptly walked out, "I won't hear of it," she had said, as she closed the large doors behind her.

And now what? Her departure left him strangely unmoved. Maybe he was even pleased. Was his request for her to consider a divorce an unconscious ruse for her to put an end to the relationship? She was really becoming a bit of a bore. He admitted she was delicious in bed. When she was willing to get into it, that is. Lately she was becoming more and more reluctant to take off her elegant clothes. She wanted to talk, she said. She wanted him to describe minutely every sensation he had when he made love. Her interest was not scientific. It was rather pornographic. Every detail was significant to her–even the feelings a man had when he unzipped his trousers or when he touched his penis during lovemaking. The ordinary questions, such as did he masturbate now then or when, were there too. It was becoming rather trying. Too bad she had missed Tiresias' opportunity. She would have loved at least once to have been entirely male. It really was trying. It was not discourse he wanted but intercourse, even, he had to admit, love. He believed he really loved the woman. Five years is a long time, even when every meeting is secret, busily arranged for, perhaps, in fact, because each meeting was prepared for so tediously and in advance.

He was thirty-two; she, thirty. He was becoming dissatisfied with his life in New York. Yet he really had no other place to go. Where other than in New York could an art dealer go? Of course there was Los Angeles, but he had a special aversion to California artists. They seemed offensive to him, too eager to make it in New York despite their propaganda to the contrary. His collectors were here, and his own roster of living artists (his gallery actually specialized in nineteenth-century American art), though few were beginning to come through strong on the scene. He himself was one of the first to push the New Realism, and he was interested in the careers of one or two of the younger artists who seemed to have a fresh approach to the figure without all those trompe l'oeil dismal magic realist effects. Yet he was going to see a California artist today in a studio on Wooster Street she was renting or subletting during her stay here. Yes, New York was meaningful to him, after all. In fact, he was negotiating for a gallery in SoHo to have a place to show some of the more daring of the younger artists who were a little too wild as yet for his uptown gallery. No, New York was his home.

And should it be a New York without a Lucy?

The opening of the door returned him to the immediate Lucy. "I think you ought to leave," she said. "My husband is due back from Greece any minute, and the governess wants to show me some of Clara's arithmetic."

"Lucy, won't you reconsider? Don't you think this illusion of domestic bliss has gone on long enough? For god's sake, divorce John and let's start a real life together."

"John," she said, and this time the absurdity of their having the same name made him tense. "John, why are you suddenly insistent on the divorce? Things have been going along so fine. Clara and Frederick need the security of having me here with John. I can't break up. I told you I never would. I always told you that this arrangement makes everything about me stronger, my marriage . . ."

"Your marriage! You know sometimes you can be a downright whore." (He noticed she did not even blanch.) "That a liaison makes your marriage stronger is a rather stupid thing to say to me, you know. Am I your lover only to cement your marriage? You know, I think I *will* leave."

Her hand was on his arm. "John," she said, "you know I love you. You know how much you mean to me."

"No, I don't."

Color seemed to slowly fade from her face as she dropped her hand from his arm. A stranger might have thought her stunned or frightened, but he knew that her color would return quickly. She would be again the distant, aloof Swiss-American, who would say, as she now did: "Oh yes, it is better for you to go. Call me whenever you wish. I'll be here."

He walked out with a certain relief, but he knew that relief would be momentary. There would be a sense of terrible loss, a kind of transfiguration of his senses. He would be stunned, lonely. He would look at old address books but would not use them. He would plunge into new projects. Luckily he was negotiating for that new SoHo gallery. All right. The separation might work. He would visit that California sculptor right away. What was her name? June LeBrun. A godawful name, with a built-in rhyme. And she was working with plinths of wood that she said she simply lined up against a wall, preferably plaster, to achieve an effect of randomness. It was a new kind of mandala, she said. Instead of concentricity to achieve mystery, there was the simple length. Occasionally, she said, she lay the lumber diagonally, as if to cut the air. It emphasized the sanctity of space (her words) and man's brutal defacement of it (again her words). Was she an artist of integrity, or simply another kind of whore. Keeping her arrangements as if they were art, part of a tradition, yet defying that tradition through the use of the outside, nonfamilial intruder? Her anti-art was probably more boring than most, but perhaps he should show a California artist. It would be just the right beginning for his new SoHo quarters, and if her pieces weren't large enough, he was sure she wouldn't mind at all having her lumberyard make up other lengths to fit the wall schemes.

June LeBrun was young, no more than twenty-two. (At this time in art history, he thought wryly, ready for a retrospective.) Pretty, deftly careless yet elegant in her blue jeans, she came to greet him at the door with rather heavy pieces of wood, as if she were already bringing her show to him, at once. She put them down, however, and led him into the large loft. "You know I'm only subletting the place until the sculptor Kenneth John comes back. His show will be closing in Los Angeles in two weeks. I'll have to decide then whether to remain longer or return directly to California."

He guessed the decision lay with him. Would he or would he not give her a show? If he gave her a show he'd have his decision regarding a SoHo gallery made for him too. He'd have to sign the lease. The idea began to seem pleasant as he glanced quickly at the sunlit studio and remembered the large rooms of the new gallery he was considering, located in the same building as the SoHo Castelli gallery. As he looked out of the loft window, he was suddenly struck by an immense shadow shimmering along the walls of the building directly opposite from them. For no reason, he remembered Leonardo's words: "I recall as one of my earliest memories that while I was in my cradle a vulture came down to me, and opened my mouth with its tail, and struck me many times with its tail against my lips." It was as if the moving shadow on the opposite wall was recapitulating the movement of the bird's tail between the infant Leonardo's lips and his own. He saw the vulture in the shadow and felt the blow upon his lips at the very moment that two pigeons flew near the loft windows. He was still trying to survive the shock of the three simultaneous experiences when he heard the girl say, in her direct Californian accents, "May I show you some of my work now?"

He had expected to see only pieces of lumber resting along the white plaster wall. Whether his recollection of Leonardo's vulture fantasy or the moving shadow or even the appearance of the pigeons had shocked him into a weakening sense of reality or whether actually before him were large black wings crudely crafted out of wood, for the moment he could not say. As the artist pointed to the sweeping arc of the wing against the wall, she made some comment about *mother* and *vulture,* and to his horror took out of a cabinet a huge black stuffed bird that looked very much like the usual reproduction of Poe's raven.

She was explaining to him that she had decided to discard her original planks of wood for the greater symbolic force of black wings. At least the arc, she was saying, was more suggestive of the actual circle of the mandala and would stimulate the viewers to contemplate more immediately the very source of their inner energies, namely, infinity and the mystery of the whole. The stuffed bird apparently was only there to show him how she originally had conceived of the idea.

As she was explaining this last point to him, she put the bird back in the cabinet and asked the art dealer what he thought about her work. Before he had time to answer, she was pointing to the opposite wall where at least there were actually planks of wood, unpainted, lying against her white plaster wall. At this point, they had the beauty of the ordinary. He almost moaned his approval, so totally relieved was he of the bleakness of his previous experience. She looked a bit unhappy at his sign of approval, for, as she was explaining, she was discarding this work entirely now and did not want to show it. She was only interested in her black wings. It was all getting to be too much for him and he asked her whether she could offer him a drink. She said she only had some sherry but she would be happy to get it for him.

While she went to what was the kitchen end of the loft, he decided to have another look at the wings. As he looked at the upper right wing of the arc, he saw what could only be a very large eyeball in a pool of deep red blood that had obviously been painted. The eyeball itself seemed real, but he couldn't figure out its huge size. From what animal, bird or beast, could so large an eyeball have been taken?

When she handed him the drink, he inquired about the eyeball only to be redirected to the entire configuration of the black wing against the wall. The eyeball was obviously something she did not wish to talk about. But it was the only thing that interested him in the entire piece – the eyeball itself, its position on the wing, and the painted pool of blood. But the interest was not aesthetic. From the aesthetic point of view there was nothing to hold the eye of the viewer. The wing was crudely crafted, the blackness of the color added somehow to its crudity, and there was no real idea behind the work. A wing against a wall symbolized nothing. It could hardly be the work of a conceptual artist. No particular documentation could make the thing interesting. Perhaps a bleeding bird wing against a wall could suggest a form of entropy, but that was rather farfetched. The eyeball on the wing, however, was a surreal gesture, but was so ineptly placed, so unimaginatively conceived that it simply lacked aesthetic appeal. Nor because of its surreal aspect could it come under the label anti-art. And it was surely not Dada. It had the mystery of a kind of personal totemism. Or maybe the mystery was even simpler than that: where did the eyeball come from? How did the artist obtain it? It was obviously not a crafted image. It had come directly from some living object.

As he sipped his sherry and considered all these questions he kept looking at the eyeball. For a single moment it seemed to him that he saw it flicker. He looked at the artist to see whether she too had noticed. Sherry had never done that to him before. She was pointing now to the space between the bottom of the piece and the wall. She said it had some aesthetic significance. This was not a work that could be put down carelessly next to the wall, she said. The measurement of exactly six-and-a-half inches from the wall must be adhered to.

Just as he was about to ask her why she was so firm about the placement, the telephone rang and she excused herself with a light gesture of her hand. What amazed him was that the hand in that quick gesture had the sweep of a wing. Furthermore, he was almost certain that on the upper right part of the hand-wing was an eyeball in a pool of blood.

At this point instead of becoming frightened he became irritated with himself and his newly nurtured fantasy world of vultures, ravens, hand-wings. He turned again to the black wing next to the wall for reassurance but this time almost cried out as he noticed that the eyeball not only flickered but actually moved at least an inch farther along the wing. He decided that when June LeBrun returned he would demand an explanation. In the meantime he kept watching as the eyeball now moved slowly back to its original position, flickered once more, and then remained quiet, as if it had been fixed there permanently.

When he heard steps approaching, he turned to ask his question. Instead of the young woman, he was now met by a tall unsavory looking young man. "Hello," the man said, extending his hand. "I'm Kenneth John. I've just returned from L.A. June offers her apologies but apparently she must take the first flight back to California. Her brother is not well."

"Good lord, Mr. John," John said, again tensing up at the sound of his own name, "isn't it rather strange for her not to say goodby?"

"But she's terribly upset, you know. Can't stand on any formalities. Surely you will excuse her."

"I suppose I'll have to, won't I," the dealer answered, as out of embarrassment he again turned to the black wing with its mysterious eyeball. "By the way, Mr. John," he managed to say, "have you noticed anything strange about this new piece of Miss LeBrun's?"

"What new piece?" asked Mr. John.

"The black wing with its wretched eyeball in a pool of blood," the dealer answered.

"Do show it to me," the artist said pleasantly. "I thought June had written me that work had already been returned to L.A."

That was too much for the New York art dealer. "What is the matter with you Californians," he cried out. "You are as shifty as your own pieces. Not an ounce of integrity in you," he said shamelessly. "June LeBrun has just asked me to show this piece, and now you tell me that it isn't here, that it is on its way to California. Can't you see it. Look," he said, pointing to what was now an empty space along the wall. "Damn," he said. "Is this sherry I'm drinking or some strange concoction that makes black wings on walls, wings on hands, and women to disappear?"

"Oh come now, Mr. er . . ."

"Farragut. John Farragut," the dealer said.

"Well, Mr. Farragut. I am sure it is not the drink. Perhaps June described the piece to you so vividly you felt as if you were actually looking at it. She has an uncanny eloquence, I know."

"So that's it," Mr. Farragut muttered. "Eloquence. Eloquence has become the new substitute for art."

"I mean her descriptions are eloquent. Her art is in her sculpture, not in her words, of course. She hopes so much that you will be offering her a show."

"I'll think about it," John Farragut said quickly. "But I must leave now. Tell Miss LeBrun that I'll be in touch with her."

As John Farragut walked toward the door, he took one backward glance at the studio, hoping to see the black wing. It was not there. Perched near the window, however, there seemed to be another bird, an enormous vulture holding in its beak what could only be the same huge eyeball now dripping in its pool of blood. He managed to get to Broadway for a cab to take him to his apartment. It was only when he was turning his key to open his door that he remembered that gouache landscape of Lucy's where in the upper right-hand corner very delicately painted was the suggestion of a vulture.

Poolside

THE POOL is quiet. Even the rain makes only slight ripples. The sheepdog, recently shorn of its thick white fur, walks slowly round the rectangular structure unaware of the young man and woman sitting close together on a bench near its edge. The man is wearing a colorful striped robe, and the woman a shiny yellow raincoat. Neither seem much concerned with the rain. Hatless they are oblivious to the dampening glow on their faces. Occasionally, however, the young man scatters the raindrops from his face with his hands but the woman is completely mindless of the rain. As she talks her lips shine with dew, and from her mouth like pebbles the drops fall. She does not care. It is a summer rain. The rain will stop, and the sun come out, their faces dry.

As the dog approaches their bench, Elise pats him, murmurs. The dog sniffs her barefoot toes and moves on along the sides of the pool. Tom takes the hand so peremptorily rejected by the dog and kisses it gently. The transition of her hand from dog to Tom unnerves her. She wonders why as she makes a circle in the sand with her right toe. Tom is silent as she forms smaller and smaller circles until intent upon a minute center she allows her toe to rest. She rather likes the taut pressure of her toe against that small center–a pressure that completely obliterates the tiny circle.

I am a small center too, she thinks, and Tom, like my big toe, obliterates me. *Why do I let him?* She removes her toe and looks closely at Tom, still silent, smiling down at her. His handsome open face with childlike dimples so near both sides of his mouth, his brown hair long enough to cover the nape of his neck, his broad shoulders like those of a football player (though he detests the game and only cares for tennis) makes him almost the All-American hero. Of course it is foolish to think of *hero* in connection with Tom, who years ago dropped out of the army into Canada and under the amnesty which he hated had returned–only to drop out of college. The only thing he knows about America, he had once said to her, is that America is Dada. He knew someone had said that in the twenties. Who, he did not know. Nor did he care. He felt words were free. Quotations were evil or institutional or something worse, and man's sayings should be plucked from anywhere to be used by anyone anywhere, and without quotes. All men were man, he would say, and all women, woman. Man was man and woman woman: each independent, yet dependent one upon the other. He reduced everything to simple terms. She did not like him less for that although at times his anti-intellectualism annoyed her and his hatred of academic life embarrassed her. After all, she was a young Ph.D. who had just gotten an appointment to a prestigious university.

Yet Tom was the All-American boy maybe just because he embodied so much of American's own querulous, if not reactionary hatred for anything bookish and academic. She is reminded of the subject of her dissertation, the American painter Whistler, whose exile from America itself led to his enormous influence on modernist art. Because he turned away from America, to orientalism, in fact, his antagonism toward the academy bore marvelous fruit.

But is Tom anything other than destructive as he works here and there around the country only occasionally finding some cabinetmaking that more or less fits into something constructive–at least she tells herself that in his carpentry he is the artist, the nonconformist who is making rather than destroying. When she patted the dog she expected nothing in return. When she offered her hand to be kissed by Tom she expected that kiss to seal something affirmative, even if it was a momentary seal of affection – a whole love. She wanted him to love all of her, her involvement with the academy too.

"I'm going in," she hears him say. "The rain has stopped. Come on."

"I don't want to," she says more harshly than she realizes. "I'll watch you," she adds to soften her words, knowing full well he has not heard her. He is an excellent swimmer and it is good to watch him push forward in his own strong fashion. "Like Hofmann's push and pull," she thinks, but quickly rebukes herself for being so academic. But were Hofmann and all his disciples academic? God, to use references from the past, a past that in itself was rebellious, revolutionary, today becomes staid and academic. How to live, how to live. Maybe she won't accept the appointment and travel along with Tom in his old Volkswagen to California. Here in Virginia they had arrived at least part of the way. In what a staid area though. And she can't even confess to Tom that she loves the friendliness and hospitality of their hosts, old friends of the family, who are gracious enough to allow them to visit without asking any questions about their nightly manipulations to pretend each has slept in his own bed. Tom isn't averse to playing that game either. It is her in bed, he wants, and he gets that.

"Elise, what's the matter? Come on in for a swim. You look positively morbid sitting there looking at your big toe. Come on in – I want to give it a bite."

Elise slowly takes off her raincoat as she feels Tom's eyes upon her body. Through his eyes she feels his love. His look makes her ache. She jumps into the pool but eludes his efforts to grab her, only for a moment though, for soon he is throwing her up in the air and biting the toe that has made the circle in the sand. She laughs as he bites it again. Finally she escapes and races him round the pool, shivering with pleasure.

In the car that evening on the way to a local drive-in, he again takes her hand, places it on his lips, and kisses it gently. Again the gesture unnerves her. She feels it strange that the hand that holds the wheel takes her own hand for a kiss. What is the matter with her anyway? There are all kinds of things on earth–dogs, car wheels, lips. Hands are everywhere. They're used in all sorts of ways. Didn't Whistler use his hands to hold a brush? Doesn't she use her hand to comb her hair, wash a dish, write a letter, to make love? Affection and use. Love and domesticity. Reality and art. Is she asking too much of Tom? Love comes easily to him. She knows his cabinetwork is mediocre. What of it, if the hand that lifts hers to his lips is a hand that is not a craftsman's, nor an artist's? Tom Walton is a man whose career is to shun careers, to enjoy the moment and the land. He is not going to become part of the establishment, and if she wants him she will have to take him as he is–anti-establishment, anti-academy, anti-booklearning. Anti anti anti. She wants to forget that he even hates Whistler though at least he does like Cézanne and can spend hours looking at a single painting of the French artist.

"There you go again," she hears him say. "What's got into you today? That faraway look. Aren't you happy? You were happy in the pool."

She doesn't answer him but places her hand on his thigh and smiles. He seems to accept the gesture and bends down and kisses her on the head.

Now it's the head, she thinks. The hand and the head. I suppose it's only natural. Anyway, he's kissed me everywhere. What is the matter with me. Tom's right. There is something wrong, and I am not happy. And besides my head hurts. "I have a headache," she blurts out, surprising him.

"For god's sakes. So what. You say it as if you've just lost your water bag. What's eating you. Say, are you pregnant or something?"

Now she really pouts and looks glum. "I don't want to go to the movies. I hate drive-ins. Let's go to a bar. I think I saw one a few miles back."

"All right, spoilsport. We'll have a drink, if that will help." He drives ahead a few feet until he can easily make the turn. She loves the way he turns the car around. Now he holds her thigh, grunting about her jeans. "What's the matter with a miniskirt?" He grins, showing the two dimples.

"Didn't take any, and besides it's a bit chilly. Don't you like me in jeans?"

"No, not in a car."

She gets that achy feeling again, and she knows that Tom holds her in his power.

She even likes the way he orders drinks. Smooth, capable–in restaurants, bars, and cars. And it isn't that he didn't do well in school. He got A's in philosophy and math in his junior year, the last year of his college attendance. And he knows more about such things as structuralism, physics, and phenomenology than she ever will. Instead of studying, he reads. Instead of writing term papers, he reads. Instead of attending lectures, he reads. He is a reader and a lover. What more does she want. She knows. She knows. She wants him to have a job. A job her parents will approve of. It has come to that! She who for four years refused to go home Christmas and Thanksgiving to face the empty ceremonials with her empty but devoted parents now wants their acceptance of her lover. It has come to that.

"Want another?" he is saying. "Say, you with the glum look. Want another?"

"Another what?"

"Another fuck."

"Yes," she says and they both laugh.

Grope

I LIGHT THE MATCH and watch the flame shoot up and the stick slowly burn. I hold it as long as I can until there is a slight glow on the stick near my thumb. As I feel the warmth I let go and black thick embers fall into the sink. I walk away. Return. My hand shakes. I take another match. This time I do not allow the flame to eat the whole match. When the flame reaches the center I smother it quickly in the sink. I let the wet stick with black tip rest. I take another match. Another and another. Never letting the stick burn to cinders. I realize the sink is too big. I'll never fill it with half-burned matchsticks. Not today anyway. It would take a year at least. Or a week. Or ten days. I go to the porch. I hear the whippoorwill. I listen as the pitch changes. I ignore the whippoorwill. I listen for the bobwhite. His chirping is less distinct. He is not close. But I listen. Listen. I return to the whippoorwill. The bird is easier to hear. Pleasanter. And his sentences are longer. Yes, sentences. Sometimes he chops them off. And shyly, embarrassed, starts them again. His syntax is consistent. His pitch has variation. But consistent. I walk down from the porch. I look for him. I look and look. I cannot find him. I still hear his cry, his statement. I listen again. He has few broken sentences. Has he found his mate? Said his say? He has flown away. Changed his course. Will he return? Will he repeat his statement? His monologue? Leave? Mate? Fly away? Now? Will he return today? Tomorrow? He will not wait for next summer. He will return soon.

I return. To the porch. Haze is over trees. I look out. I hear two short notes. I listen to the pause between them. It is the bobwhite again. He is more subtle. Deeper. Less nervous. But he is gone. Again. Ah, he speaks. Two short studied notes. Silence. Everything silent. I am silent too. I listen to my heart. I can't hear it. I place my hand above it. I cannot find my heart. I stand up. Sit down. Place my hand on my heart. Still cannot find it. I know I am breathing. I stand up. Place my hand on my heart. I find that pumping instrument. I hold my hand there. I sit down. I hold it firmly against my heart. I hear its statement, quick, regular. Mechanical. A sound without heart. No heart in my heart. Yes. No orchestration. I take my hand away. I am saddened. At the very core; existence, the heart, no heart. I pick up my left hand, place the thumb of my right hand on my pulse. Beat Beat Beat. The heart in the pulse. No heart. I am saddened. I stand up. I walk down from the porch. I look up. I raise my head. I look at the old magnolia tree. Its leaves are heavy, wide. I see only two flowers on low branches. Aching white. They are still. Waiting to die. Above no flowers. They have fulfilled their promise. Of death. I watch the process. Of their dying. I watch. I see nothing. It is invisible. I am sad. I cannot see death's process. I return to the porch. I sit down. I am on the rocker. I am speedier than the rungs of the rocker. My mechanical heart is a faster runner. My heart is a winner. It is faster. I rock harder and harder. I almost topple. I rock faster and faster. My heart pounds harder. It is winning winning. It can win a race. I slow down on my rocker. I place my feet squarely on the porch floor. The rocker stops almost in midair. I feel my heart again. It is pounding pounding, my mechanical heart. I win.

De l'Essence

THE SUN bore down upon her. It was low, crouching. Bright orange. She was in a field. No houses. No dogs. No people. One long stretch of road. Once there were people. Maybe yesterday. Maybe two hours ago. Now, she, alone, standing, the sun with her crouching. Where was she to go, if not here. Here. Alone. Standing. All that had been, was. Was, with him, with child, with those strange plucking parents, who devoured. Now all that was had been. Here, she, alone. Standing. It was hot, here, now. The sun, too low. She remarked, I am here. Alone. With shoes, dress, bra, no panties. The stockings lie near me. Torn. Ripped off. With shoes on. How? It doesn't matter. My legs are bruised. Blood on the thigh. Oozing. Fingers soothe thighs. Smooth the oozing. Make a pretty spot: round, edges, irregular. Water would be good. Water here? Impossible. Hardly any water in Oklahoma. Faucets sometimes leak. In houses. Houses? Not here. Alone. Nothing. Grass. Grass, even yellow, is company. A blade of grass. The world: one everyone all. Dust to dust. Grass to grass. Pot. Grass. Yellow grass. Odors, musty foreign forlorn fornication. Him? Child. No. Parents too devouring. Plucking parents. Now I lay me down to sleep. Grass sparse. Not comfortable. Sun burning. Dress could protect eyes. Dress of wool. White. Like a turban is the dress as she takes it off. Always was artistic. Even a faded ribbon on her hair gave her character. Now a dress-turban. White. Protective custody. Child? Him. Yes. Alone. She bruising. Thighs pretty in red swirls. Slowly. It takes time to die. Alone. Even here. Alone. No houses. Car tracks on the road. Recent too. Even the smell of gasoline. Always hated that. Him? Maybe. Yesterday? Today or then or two hours ago. Not now. Now peace. The sun lowing. Tiger tiger burning bright. In the fields of Oklahoma. Water soothing. Hydrotherapy. Hydrophobia. Therapy, madness. All the one the one the many grass a blade grass all like leaves falling down falling down. Would he return? With water with hydrophobia? Was it help he wanted? No, she wanted help. From him from child from devouring parents. Plucking. Yes he said stay here stay right here lie down wait it won't take long a gas station. *Où y a-t-il un poste d'essence? La route est-elle bonne? Pouvez-vous m'indiquer un bon mécanicien?* Here. To wait. *Pour l'essence?* Yes, right down to it, the very essence. That essential moment when he the child the devouring parents. Marry! Marry! Him? For the child, they said. For the child. The sun was terrible crouching burning orange. Orange dishes orange kitchen orange chairs. Blue is his favorite color. Always works, he says. Soothing. Like the sea. Sea-surge. The surging waters. Water? Hydrotherapy hydrophobia. Yes, she remarked aloud. I am thirsty the sun is too hot crouching sun. Stockings like snakes lying. Near me. Ripped off. How? Toward what road to what town to what garage in nowhere? The car has problems, he said. Problems. Then why use it, she said. Got to. Have not other. Have you child new job. It will break down if it's no good, she said. Sure it might he said. But we've got to try. To get there. At least get there, he said. Reassuringly. The baby cried reassuringly. The last gasp to the garage in NOWHERE. She visiting on the grass pleasant sight turbaned mother relaxed waiting for *l'essence* in nowhere reassuringly blood trickling down unstockinged feet in nowhere listening to no birds to no wind but remembering the distant sound of a lonely horn it takes time to die.

Picasso's Goat

IT BEGAN on the tennis court. He was wearing a white T-shirt, with the inevitable alligator, and white shorts. His Nike sneakers, leather, looked good on his big feet. His long legs, long body gave him presence. His face was weatherbeaten from his frequent solitary walks around the countryside, walks consciously taken to turn his libido into love for nature–though nature in this part of the country consisted chiefly of pokeweed, sagebrush, and stones. Middle age had left its mark on his face. It was beginning to be lined, and his hair had turned almost completely gray. But middle age gave him no respite from sexual longing.

His wife, now tight-lipped, was no longer eager. She lay in their bed, and slept. Where was that old delight? Desire was still in him. Yes, he lusted. Now and then a beautiful student stirred him. Glances were not enough. As he held his tennis racket in his hand that Thursday afternoon, that hand felt hard. It was anticipating. He had come alone to the court, again anticipating. Last week at the farthest end of the campus court where the fence met the street of ugly, one-story homes, without benefit of yard or grass, in front, behind or on their sides, he had seen her playing with another student. He had watched her legs move gracefully and her hand, as she lifted the racket to meet the fast-moving ball, flutter like a sure hawk beating down on its prey. He watched her movements for ten minutes until once when she put down her racket to tie her laces their eyes met. She smiled. He still felt the warmth of that smile, even its beckoning. He had left the court then, his heart lifted up as her hand. It seemed to him a smile hovered on his lips for hours afterwards.

As he now walked slowly toward that same court he felt like a sixteen-year-old wanting to wish on some talisman for his love to appear. He was closer now. It was the same time only one week later when her graceful swinging body had been playing on the far court. As he looked now he saw a figure alone, pacing the clay court with her racket in her hand. What a miracle, he thought, as he quickened his pace. She was clearly waiting for her partner to appear. Her eyes were searching his very approach. Suddenly she saw him. He was close enough to see the smile on her lips. That same desire, that same beckoning appeared. He did not waver. Though his heart seemed to be racing, he walked as casually as he could with his own smile wearing an equal warmth. He said *hello.*

"Hello. Do I know you?" she asked. "You do look familiar, and yet . . ."

"I teach English at the college. I saw you playing here last week. I liked the way you hit the ball. May I join you in a warmup?"

"I'm waiting for Mary, my partner, but I suppose while waiting it wouldn't hurt to warm up. OK," she said.

He walked to the other end of the court. She began with an unsettling thrust of her hand. He hit the first ball, the second, and the third. Suddenly he was running all over the court. Every ball seemed a perfect hit. She swung faster and faster. He could hardly bear the pace. He swerved the ball, low, teasingly, hardly over the net. She got it. He tried farther out. She got that too. It was not a game of tennis. It was their first temptation. It was all foreplay. Two lovers holding back playing furiously, waiting for their final thrust.

Suddenly the girl stopped short. *Mary,* she said. *Mary, there you are. Good.* He was out of breath. His lust still on the very edge.

"Hello," he said to Mary, when the girl herself out of breath, blushing, introduced him.

"I know you. I had you for freshman composition. Two years ago. I'm a junior," Mary added.

"Oh. But of course I remember you. Mary Esposito? The girl who sat in the back row always talking to what-was-his-name John Harris?"

"Yes." She wasn't at all embarrassed. "Yes, that's me. You know, English is a bore. Don't you think so?" She turned to the girl. But *she* was embarrassed. "Well, I don't know. I suppose it depends on who is teaching it." She looked at him squarely in the eye as if to say, *you would never be boring.*

He laughed. "I agree with you, Mary. English grammar is a bore, and I suppose it's particularly boring in the course. Yes, it's a bore. I can't deny that."

They seemed relieved at his admission. "But I mustn't keep you two from your game. By the way, what's your name?" He turned to the girl whose eyes averted his.

"Gladys. Gladys Sterne," she said to a passing cloud.

"A good name," he said. "A good name. I like the first syllable: *glad.* Are you usually 'glad'?"

"But that's not a good name for her at all," Mary quickly interrupted. "Not at all. I can't remember when Gladys was 'glad.' Am I right, Gladys?"

Mary's insensitivity made Gladys blush again. "Well, well, I don't know. Let's start our game. And thank you. Thank you for the good tennis. Really good."

"Well, then we must play again. Do you ever come here on Tuesdays? I can't always make it on Thursdays, even though I seem to have been able to do it two weeks in a row. Meetings and things, you know. Can you be here on Tuesday at three?"

"Yes, I can. That is, if my mother won't need me." Mary and she exchanged glances. "If my mother won't need me," she repeated.

"Fine. I'll be here on Tuesday, at three. If you don't come, I'll understand that you were needed." He looked at her, and for the first time noticed something strange about her mouth, a kind of drooping quality that he had once noticed on a cousin of his shortly before she was taken to a hospital. The hospital never did much for her frequent nervous breakdowns. He dismissed his little shock of ominous recognition and took her hand to say good-by. Her hand was as warm as his. He felt a shiver and twitch in his groin. He turned quickly to Mary and shook her hand as well. A different gesture, a slight polite shaking of the hand. As he walked away he felt two eyes burning through him. He felt that shiver again. It made him happy—and sad. He was not thinking of his wife at all. He knew the sadness was empathic. He felt bound to Gladys in some strange—was it neurotic?—way. Was her sadness a mere reflection of his own? Was it lust now or another kind of attraction? Was his desire being displaced by another kind of lure? Should he return on Tuesday? It would not be fidelity that would hold him back, but a strange foreboding of something more devastating, corrosive. Gladys's lips. My god, her lips. What did those unpretty tight contortions hold for him? His own story? The hidden foulness of an unnameable disease? A contemporary disease: loathsome, contagious. Its source: the malignancy of a civilization bent on its own destruction. His desire to follow that mouth was as corrupt, as insidious as armies into Vietnam, into El Salvador. It had nothing to do with adultery, infidelity. It was a longing for death. A longing to sleep side by side with the ill, the diseased, the mind unbetrothed to truth, to a future.

Oh, he was a pompous ass. An unsuccessful English professor turning his life into symbols or into a novel he would never write.

As he shaved before the bathroom mirror that next Tuesday morning, he watched his mouth as it tightly closed. His mouth did not yet show signs of his own malignancy. He closed his eyes and in a strange hallucination saw Gladys's lips moving like a serpent over his own body. He opened his eyes and wanted to retch. The vision remained with him for moments longer. It was only a knocking on the door that shocked him out of his nausea. "Hurry," his wife was saying. "Don will be picking you up in five minutes. Don't keep him waiting again, for goodness sake."

The mention of Don's name returned him to his senses. Not his wife's voice. Certainly not her voice, that voice that once had beguiled him and now made him think of scorpions, or at least of his grandmother's knitting needles. There he was again, the old prof, thinking of silly symbols. He had better relate his snake analogies to Gladys, Gladys with the drooping serpentine lips. Fortunately, Don's sanity would call him back. Stop him from making morbid symbology of lips and desire. He was just a bored English teacher using critical jargon even on a tennis court, even thrusting it onto his own desires. Wasn't he just a middle-aged man looking for a last fling, a fling with a young body, desiring, desirous, covetous, coveting? His new equation should not be an old metaphor of a fallen Eden. There was no serpent. He hadn't noticed an apple. And there was no Eve. Mouths, drooping or not, were mouths to feed, to kiss, to long for. Why was he courting some mythological, even demonic disaster. Wasn't the risk of seduction, right here on campus, of a young student, wasn't that enough? All those lawsuits brought by women students were already making a mess of male professors' lives. What was he looking for! He took his towel, marked "his" (of course, in a home run by an efficient middle-class, let alone middle-aged wife) from the rack and patted his face. He gave one long searching look into the mirror. Saw that his own lips were neither serpentlike nor especially gluttonous, and closed the bathroom door with a strange gentleness. What was he caressing? What episode was he so gingerly closing off? As he descended the stairs lightly quickly feeling strong young in his whole body he pushed aside the academic notion of a descent into hell. He was still in his own house. The house with a wife, with a child, when she was not in college. Walls walls everywhere of security–though of boredom, of a quotidian stillness that was defeating him even in the classroom. Didn't Mary say his course was dull? And when would he be able to turn a classroom into excitement if he only taught freshman composition and an introduction to fiction? A middle-aged associate professor with only a textbook to his credit. But this new passion? Would it make him productive again? Would his long-overdue unfinished book on D. H. Lawrence have a new appeal to him? If Gladys complied, that is. If her body were as delicious in bed as on the courts. But he was certainly running ahead of things . . .

Good old Don, ever faithful. "You know we're late, don't you, Carl? Late. Ten minutes late already. And we're not even in the car. Do you think the old dean will be pleased? I can't stand that contemptuous smile he gives us every time we come in late."

The dean's smile too. Snakelike? Into what doom, toward what devil did Dean Simpson's smile lead him? "OK, Don. Here I am. Never more ready to listen to the monotonous tones of William K. Simpson, dean of Elmira College in the hills of Tennessee, far away from the temples of Arcady, set right down here in the Bible Belt of America. Bye, Margaret. See you tonight. Say, Don, do you and Marilyn want to come back for dinner?" he asked after brushing Margaret's cheek in good-by. Was it his snake's lips, fangs of his own demons? She looked accusingly at him. This woman, his wife, who after his daughter had left for college, had become a college secretary, to be "involved," she had said to him, "involved in the world's work." Of course she didn't want another couple for dinner. She would not have time to do the necessary additional shopping. All she saw, it was clear, were more dishes in the dishwasher, the need for a more elaborate dinner, a late evening and the consequent difficulty of getting up in time for work. He could see in her accusatory eyes that she felt abused again. Her taut lips said silently (ah, how well he knew her!): *You selfish beast—all for the sake of a beer-drinking evening.* He almost felt Margaret's sigh of relief when Don said, "No. This is Marilyn's anthro night. You know she's taking that course with John Davison."

"Oh, right. I forgot. OK, some other time. We're off, Margaret." Again he almost heard that sigh of relief.

Carl enjoyed the discussion of changing course numbers. The absurdity of it all when his own mind was filled with scorpions, strange drooping mouths, his own heartbeats, desires rising, and the hideous symptoms of his heated symbologies. At one nightmarish moment he was sure he saw a Salvadoran guerrilla with a mouth like Gladys's, and the next he heard again Mary's boorish remark: "But that's not a good name for her at all. I can't remember when Gladys was *glad.*"

"If you have a zero in front of the new numbers," Betty Ryan was saying. He hardly heard the rest but he did look at her mouth as she was speaking. Betty Ryan, surely not more than thirty-three, yet dry, reeking with varieties of new course numbers. Another efficient Margaret. She might even find her Carl–or was her Carl embedded in the new college catalogue that she wanted to change. He looked around, not hearing words, sentences, little high-pitched sounds of laughter. All he saw were mouths speaking, quiet, close-lipped. Old mouths of satiety. Young mouths clamping down on desire. Middle-aged mouths too tired to suggest a thing. And then in his own mind's eye the mouth of Gladys: desiring, covetous, but drooping, with the contemporary disease: madness! Yes, that was it. Her mouth contradicted the teasing pleasures of her tennis game. The girl was sick. He now tried to remember that thin body, those especially thin legs. She probably was not eating well. Food was distasteful to her. So it was with his cousin before her first hospital stay. He remembered Gladys's blushes again, and the always drooping mouth. And what about that mother? What story did that mother hold?

"Do you agree, Carl?" Simpson was asking. "We need your vote too, you know. This is too small a department not to have a consensus. What do you think?"

Undaunted, Carl answered cheerfully: "I agree. It's fine with me." He could almost hear Betty Ryan's sigh of relief. Sounded just like Margaret's too. Tennessee had already smothered her, turned her breath into sighs. Sighs heard or unheard, they were always there.

Finally, afternoon. He was waiting at the tennis court. He felt good. Even powerful. He was keeping his hallucinations under control. He would allow no interference. Even if his game would be only a game of tennis. He'd enjoy that. Soon he saw Gladys walking slowly toward the court. She was not carrying her racket. Hm. What was she planning. Wasn't it his game, his pace? Her walk seemed awkward now. Those lithe tennis legs lagged. It was as if she were finding only stones along her path. She was looking down, almost searching for something. When she finally arrived, close enough to touch him, she looked up at him with that peculiar mouth and said: "Sorry, I can't play today. Can't stay long at all. Must get back to my mother, but I had to let you know that I wanted to come." With the word *wanted* she blushed and smiled. Her smile lasting only a moment was a lover's smile he thought: its warmth relieved him. He forgot serpentine analogies. His interpretation of her state had been mad. He was the crazy one. "Perhaps we can just talk," he said. He leaned against the fence. She went toward it too, not leaning on it, but allowing her right hand to touch it, almost to play upon it as if it were an instrument. Her nervousness played its own tune. She waited for him to speak. He kept looking at her. But someone had to speak. He was older, the professor. He began. "Is your mother ill? Why does she need you so much?"

Her eyes were frank even as her mouth drooped. "Yes, how did you know. She is ill. Mentally. She's in and out of the hospital. She's been home now for a month. There is no one to be with her. My father, well, he left my mother many years ago. There's only me. I've got to watch over her." She uttered the words as if she were a child reciting a Longfellow poem she had been forced to memorize. There were no changing tones in her description of her family life.

"Oh, I see. I'm very sorry."

"No need to be sorry," she said. "Everything has reasons, and everything leads to something, I suppose. Good or bad. Chiefly leads to nothing in particular. Yes, nothing in particular."

"Oh no. I don't think so. Look, your own difficulties turned you to tennis. I met you here. I don't think that nothing in particular. I think that rather special, don't you?"

Was she going to open that mouth of hers in amazement? No, she kept it shut firmly, scrupulously, allowing those uneven curling lips to take their usual shape. "I must go now," she said, in the same monotone.

"I'll walk you home. I gather you live nearby?"

"Yes, I live nearby."

They walked in silence. Soon she was pointing. "You see that yard with the old bicycle wheels and broken-down car engines, tires and things. That's my yard. My father used to be a junk dealer. This is all that's left of him. A nice legacy, isn't it," she said with bitterness. He said nothing, but he touched her arm in sympathy. He withdrew it quickly. He knew the gesture said too little. They came to her front door, its surface streaked with old peeling white paint. Patches of paint still clung to the bleak brass knob as if even the painter knew years ago that everything in and out of this house was tumbledown.

"Would you like to come in?" she asked.

"Yes," he said. He followed her through the dark corridor. She brought him into a damp, small kitchen. "My mother," she said, pointing to what looked like an old woman in a shawl. He looked at the mouth. It was Gladys's: a drooping, serpentine, curling mouth. "Professor Ryder," she said to her mother. "He walked me home."

"Tea, give him tea," the mother said without looking at him. She was sitting near the window. Her view was the junk on the ground that may once have been a lawn. Probably not in Gladys's lifetime.

"Would you like some?" Gladys looked up at him, trying to smile.

"No, not really. No, thank you," he said.

"I wish I had taken your course," she said as she sat down opposite him. The table looked unclean. A plastic tablecloth, originally green, now tattered and almost colorless, was spread over what was probably a wooden table.

"What course?" he asked as if he had a variety, as if he had not taught composition and the introduction to fiction for years and years.

"Your introduction to fiction. I've heard your lectures are exciting. Exciting. Very visual too. And that's wonderful for an art major like me. And a friend of mine heard you speak on Lawrence. Something about a horse episode. She said you made everything symbolic. Exciting."

He laughed. "Yes, I guess I make everything symbolic!" He tried not to look at her demonic, drooping mouth. He tried to brush away thoughts of serpents and scorpions. "Do you ever think in terms of symbols?" he asked. "Look at me. What am I symbolic of?"

She looked. She looked closely at his face. He felt her eyes pierce him. He felt they singed his skin. What was she seeing? "Yes," she said. "I see symbols in your face. A symbol."

"What symbol?"

"I won't tell. I won't tell."

"That's unfair. Really, that's unfair. When I discuss Lawrence's symbols, I explain what they mean to me. Come now. Tell me what symbol you see on my face. *What* symbol?"

Her face became immobile. She looked bewitched. She was white marble, a white marble speaking. "I see," she said slowly, "I see–a goat. A gray scruffy goat. Picasso's goat."

His stomach turned. "A what?" Would he really retch? "A what?"

She had no time to reply. They both heard it. The disembodied voice: "There's a car stopping in front of our house. A car."

It was the mother. "It's the lady from welfare," she was saying. "I see a pad in her hand. She has a pad in her hand. I suppose she has a pencil in her bag. A pencil in her bag."

Gladys turned her face away, but quickly looked again at Carl. What was she seeing now? He was sure his face was yellow, black–no, gray. He had turned into a gray scruffy goat. Was he retching or was he bleating? "I'm sorry," she was saying. "You should never have asked me. I'm always finding animals in faces. And I like Picasso's goat. Who knows what his goat was to him?"

He felt his color coming back. He shrugged his shoulders. "Who knows what his goat is to *you?*" he said as he rose from his seat. He tried to regain his composure. "I'm sure you will want privacy. With the lady." He pointed toward the door. "I'll see you on the court next Tuesday." Was he crazy–to accept an insult, ignore welfare, madness–and invite this strange, disturbed girl to play tennis? He was enough himself, however, to take Gladys's hand to say good-by. She again turned her face away. The doorbell rang. He dropped her hand. He opened the door, nodded to the woman who was entering, and walked slowly back to the campus. His feet dragged but he was not bleating. He'd have to live with his goat, with all of his demons, and he knew that with them all he'd return to the court next Tuesday. *Ma-a-a!*

But he could not return to the court next Tuesday. His daughter, a sophomore at Northwestern, was coming home for the Easter holidays. He had to pick her up at the airport. There was no way to let Gladys know. He looked in vain for a Sterne in the phone book. There wasn't a single Sterne listed. But of course they had no phone! Dreadful to miss the appointment. Dreadful not to be able to let her know. He hoped she'd be there on the following Tuesday. He'd explain then. She would understand. No doubt she was used to disappointment. Yes, poor thing, she was used to disappointment. She would understand.

He loved picking up his daughter Elizabeth at the airport. Without Margaret. Her *Hi, Dad* was quite wonderful. Even domestic life seemed possible again. His daughter Elizabeth who was as exuberant as happy as Gladys was sad. Yes, it suddenly came to him as a shock: Gladys and Elizabeth were probably about the same age. He was pursuing his daughter! The middle-aged professor pursuing his daughter. But what a substitute. Everything inverse, if not perverse. Instead of a happy Elizabeth he was seeking a disturbed Gladys. Instead of the liveliness of Elizabeth, the strange quiet of Gladys. Instead of openness, he was seeking mystery, the mystery of disease. Of all the students on campus, why was he craving a scholarship student, bereft of simple young joy? All that contumely that lay on her lips: the shape of the disease, the reproach of it.

They were eating his favorite food, the night of Elizabeth's arrival, that Tuesday night, delicate thin slices of London broil. Margaret couldn't destroy London broil at least. Elizabeth was telling a story of her English professor who had once met the poet John Berryman. It was a story describing Berryman's genius as well as his vileness. Good and evil, Carl thought. Are they always together, always allied. He looked lovingly at his daughter, listened to her beautifully modulated lovely voice, a voice that had for years sung in the church choir. She wanted to be an actress. She was now rehearsing the role of Ophelia in her college production. Elizabeth, ah pretty Ophelia . . . *There's rosemary, that's for remembrance. Pray you, love, remember.* Carl smiled at the prospect of his Elizabeth giving or gently throwing the rosemary to a young Laertes. He was startled out of these thoughts by the ring of the telephone. Margaret was saying, "I'll tell whoever is calling that we are eating dinner." Yes, one of Margaret's many domestic rules: no one must speak during the dinner hour over the phone. "Who was it," Carl asked when she returned. "Oh, a student, I guess. I said she'd have to call you after the holidays. In the office. Rude of her to call here anyway. Isn't it, dear?" She looked at him coldly.

"What was her name?" He felt color mounting to his cheeks.

"Something like Gladys Sterne," his wife said.

"Oh." He felt his voice quiver. *(Pray you, love, remember.)* Only Elizabeth looked at him questioningly. Not so innocent after all, he thought.

"Go on with your story, Elizabeth," Margaret said.

A story about Berryman, the notorious seducer of college girls. Cruelly appropriate, Carl thought. Cruelly appropriate.

The following Tuesday Gladys was on the court. They played tennis. She asked for no explanation. He gave none. Again those nimble legs, that violent tossing of the ball, the back and forth passing in a game beyond a game. This time there was no Mary, either. They had the court to themselves. When it was over, she said she could not stay. She did not want him to accompany her home. No, she did not want to go for a cup of coffee. But when they said good-by and he took her hand, she let it linger even longer than before. When she withdrew her hand, she said, harshly, again with no emotion: *My mother is always home.* Before he could answer, her back was in front of him. She walked briskly this time. He watched her lithe legs move forward, away from him. *Pray you, love, remember.*

Elizabeth returned to college. Gladys did not. No more Tuesday tennis games. Gladys Sterne, he was told by Mary two weeks later, was in the state mental hospital fifty miles away. *Fare you well, my dove! You must sing 'A-down, a-down . . . O, how the wheel becomes it! It is the false steward, that stole his master's daughter.* Gladys Sterne was in the mental hospital, fifty miles away. Fifty miles away.

For a month Carl could not look in the mirror when he shaved. He heard too many strange noises.

Ancient Ritual

WITH HELMETS on their heads they return to the beach. Their bodies polished with grease gleam in the sun. Peering through the telescope, she thinks their nude bodies look like burnt almonds. Their helmets seem absurd to her, and so do the guns in their holsters at their sides.

They are not soldiers. Are they on location? Are they a dance group or actors, extras for some pornographic film?

She puts the telescope down and watches the loose curtain as it waves out toward the farthest corner of the large English park below her. Her blond hair tied tightly at the nape of her neck by a red ribbon gives the young woman a sense of strangulation, as if the ribbon were round her throat, tightening tightening. She can hardly breathe. Yet she once again picks up the telescope and peers through it. Again she sees the men, this time lounging on the sand, holding the flutes to their lips. She thinks she hears melodies as she watches them arranged in a semicircle, their bodies even more brilliant with grease, with sun. Her throat feels less taut as she watches.

One man stands up, removes his helmet, puts down his flute, and turns toward a man seated in the circle. He voices some command. The seated man turns away sharply even as he is knocked over by the standing man, who in a powerful embrace pummels the man sexually.

The woman trembles but does not put down her telescope. She watches as the man slowly succumbs. She thinks she hears a groan from him, a groan of pleasure and release. The telescope shakes in her hands until she cannot sustain even its light weight and has to put it down. Now she feels a tightening of the belt around her waist. It becomes almost unbearable as she stumbles to her bed and with weak hands tries to unclasp the tight buckle. Shaking, she gasps for breath. Gathering all her declining strength she makes a last attempt to ease the buckle. This time it works. Her green belt lies on the bed beneath her, the silver clasp gleaming.

She places her hands on her pounding heart. She lets them rest there until slowly she begins to breathe normally. She closes her eyes but opens them quickly to blind her from the reappearing vision of the men on the sand. She stares at the ceiling covered with painted angels, of rounded bellies, rosy cheeks, and wings that look like enlarged butterflies pinned to a scrapbook. As she looks, she relaxes. Stretching her hands upward she touches those wings until disintegrating into thin films of wax they fall lightly, covering her entire face. As she lies enjoying the caress of falling waxwings, she tries again to close her eyes. The beach scene does not reappear. She rests like a corpse receiving strange balm, beads of sweat from a priest reciting the last sacrament.

Hours pass. Suddenly she feels a fluttering upon her face as if the films of wax are moving. The sensation at first is pleasant. Her bed itself becomes a bed of feathers and her whole body rises as if it is itself down. Even as she succumbs to the delicacy of her invisible massager she becomes aware of a subtle pain upon her face. Impalpably the light flutter upon her face hardens to crystals, then to needles, and then to distinct claws ripping layers of wax film through to her own skin. The shift from gentleness to fierce tearing away of wing and flesh is so sudden that she experiences both pleasure and pain. In agony she tries to sit up in her bed but feels an enormous weight upon her face by now drenched in blood. She tries to lie face down on the pillow to protect herself from the fierce marauding but all she can do is twist her body with only one cheek protected from her enemy. Weakened by loss of blood, powerless even to cry out, she lies still in her semiprotected position. How long she lies she does not know. She has lost consciousness.

The men on the beach leave their flutes on the sand and sit tightly together in a circle. They sit like sun gods–nude, strong, each in worship of his own body, yet each admiring the others in their tight circle. One is taller, stronger than the others. His crotch is covered with a shield-like insignia of red silk. Obviously the leader, he gestures to the men to remove their helmets. In unison they raise hands and in a quick movement grasp the headgear. Arching their bodies toward their feet they place the helmets in front of extended legs. Returning to a sitting position each looks intently upon the leader awaiting further instructions. The leader remains unmoved. His face is stone. Its strange pallor contrasts with his bronzed body. Staring directly in front of him he is as indifferent to the circle of men as just a moment before he had been intent upon his command. The men hold their eyes riveted to his face. How long they remain in this taut position the only observer of the scene does not know. The man who earlier had been sexually attacked sits apart from the circle. Exhausted, still confused, still feeling at once pain and pleasure, he has withdrawn from the group and is now watching them in a lazy, half-interested fashion. The leader who had attacked him has completely dismissed the man from his view. Now nothing seems on the leader's mind as he stonelike stares ahead of him, unperturbed not only by the isolated one but by the men piercing him with their eyes awaiting his new command. That command does not come. Yet they do not remove their eyes from his face.

Minutes pass? An hour? Two? The sun beats down on their faces, indiscriminately. Upon leader. Upon isolated one. Upon the men still drawn in the circle. Silence is neither reproach nor storm, thinks the isolated one, as he begins to look with more interest toward the group. His fatigue, his sexual shock are leaving him. He is almost ready to become part of the circle, even to the extent of turning his eyes to his leader, to become transfixed in a silent unwavering obeisance. Just as this decision is taking hold of him, he hears a penetrating scream. The scream is shrill, eerie, a female voice bestial in terror. The men in the circle shudder. He notices that even the leader stands up. Involuntarily. All turn as they see the woman running toward them blood streaming down her face, a face no longer a face but planes of bone and flapping flesh. She is almost upon them when in a sudden jerky movement her body falls, completely limp.

As the men rush toward her the leader shouts, HALT. They halt, legs taut, as the isolated one slowly picks himself up, reaches for his gun and with perfect aim shoots the leader through the heart.

She Wasn't Joyce's Nora

In the beginning, she knew. And like all beginnings within it lay its end. But fortunately, as always to the experiencer of the event, the end was still unknown. Though the end was inevitable and would grow from the beginnings of that event, the miracle lay in its development–through chance. Thus the paradox: formulation known yet unknown, inevitable yet within its inevitability the working of chance, the random.

Here Nora was, standing in the middle of a large living room with an interesting arrangement of windows that transformed the room's rectangular shape into a kind of octagonal affair. The windows were not in any way or in any obvious way built in an orderly fashion. Randomly built? They seemed anyhow simply to appear–here there anywhere as if the architect's plan was based on impulse, not on order, Nora thought as she held her vodka-and-tonic glass, trying not to look too interested in the man before her. She turned toward the many colorful cushions on the sofas hugging the walls. She loved color. She loved shapes. The pillows gave her the joy of seeing both. These too had been placed without any formal order. They were thrown, as they should be, she reflected. Here and there squares and rectangles of color held the eye. As Nora looked she felt a passion that seemed to come directly from the pillows. Or was it from the vodka? Or was the passion aroused because she knew it was the beginning as she looked at the man, who had just introduced himself. There was a lilt in his voice, that lilt of the irrepressible Irish. His ruddy complexion seemed to glow more and more as she looked at him. His smile was in his eyes as well as on his lips.

"I am Jim," he said. "Jim Nigel. And you?"

"I am Nora," she replied almost picking up his lilt and smile. "Nora Smith."

"Nora Smith, a simple name. Easy to remember, a name that to an Irishman recalls Joyce. Joyce's companion, his earthy, mischievous wife Nora."

She smiled again, this time in recognition. "I read Joyce in college. Forgot him since."

"Don't forget him. Read him again. Now." He broke into a laugh. "No, don't read him. Ignore my pedagogy. No reason for you to hold on to a writer whom you want to forget. I'm what they call in university circles a Joycean. But I won't inflict my obsession on you."

Nora took another sip of vodka. "Perhaps you have other obsessions?"

His eyes sparkled. They were blue eyes embedded in pure white that said nothing, absolutely nothing. Only the blue talked. His eyes talked.

"More than one, of course. But I was divorced two years ago, and I'm obsessed, obsessed with . . . strange that I am telling you this. I'm obsessed with . . . a need . . . a need . . ."

"For a woman, any woman, of course."

"No, that is not true. Would I stand here and vulgarly declare such a need to you, a stranger, a . . . very desirable woman?"

"Yes, why not? You're declaring it now, aren't you? Your needs are natural enough." Nora sighed. Her needs too were natural enough. Too easily satisfied but on a level that always left her depressed. She looked at Jim's light brown hair. Straight, falling on his forehead. Her fantasy made leaps. *They were lovers. Quick, immediate lovers. They loved. They loved. They parted. She was depressed.*

"But you are wrong. I won't tell you my obsession."

"You've told it. You've told it," she repeated and laughed.

Their host, Dan Roberts, walked over to them. "Glad the two of you have met. You have a lot in common."

"Oh no," Nora said. "Jim is a Joycean. And I long ago left Joyce behind."

"But, Nora, you're a painter, and Jim has a passion for art, American art."

"So," Nora turned to Jim, "you're . . . obsessed with collecting, collecting art?"

He smiled. "No, I'm not a collector. You forget I'm an academic, an Irish academic at that–though, it is true, now at an American university. How can I afford collecting? Collecting is anathema to me anyway. I like to look, not to possess."

"You see," Dan said, as he turned away. "You do have something in common. Neither of you is a collector."

"Then I guess I was wrong. You are not obsessed with possessing women. You merely want to look."

"Again you are wrong. To look at a beautiful woman is a pleasure. To be able to possess her is a gift from the gods."

"But you forget. We women have been freed. Men no longer *possess* a woman, don't you know."

"I know and do not know. Love matters are too primitive to be newly devised. Courting rules may change. Maybe there is no longer any courting. But man is man. Woman, woman. Don't you think?"

Nora sighed again. "I'm afraid you are right there. That is both the joy and tragedy of life."

"Especially your life?"

"Especially yours and mine," Nora said. They both smiled. They had met. Something had been sealed.

Nora was in her apartment, one month later. They had seen each other eight times. At the moment he was obsessed. With her. And she with him. Since the end had not come, there was no depression. Would it come? Would it end? And how would it end? She had finished her breakfast ready to go downtown to her loft. There had been another beginning. A new canvas. With the very beginning her style seemed to make an abrupt change. No more graffiti, no more cartoon characters, no more overloaded canvas with strange creatures and violent colors. Her new work almost as atmospheric, as geometric as a Richard Diebenkorn's. More lines forming rectangles, suggestions of elliptical oceans and thin paint making demarcations along edges that bled. Would the change have occurred without Jim, she wondered, as she walked up the three flights of stairs to her studio. She opened the heavily hinged door and threw her coat on a chair near the entrance. She stood in the center of the large, bare room and looked hard at the new canvas stretched on a wall before her. Without figures, without graffiti, without grotesquerie. It was as if some new quiet had come upon her, but still there was some painterly need, something perhaps not so painterly, something from her guts that was making a new demand. She quickly changed into jeans and shirt and found the brush that would translate this gut feeling into a new shape, a new color. Onto the right bottom edge of the canvas and near a pale blue area she painted a red, raggedly defined circle. The red was a Francis Bacon red, harsh, unsubtle, a raging red. The contrast between the pastel colors, the quiet shapes she had already painted, and this new red irregular circle was making more than a formal statement, she knew. Never is a line only a line, a circle only a circle, a color only a color despite the Modernists and their unbending aesthetic. Even if the canvas would have no figure, what happened on the canvas was a human happening painted by a person to be felt by people who ate, worked, slept, and made love. People who made war. People who were victims and victimizers.

There must be a relationship then between her meeting (mating?) with Jim and the new quiet, with the latest new surge of Bacon red. She remembered a painting that she had recently seen by a young woman. The painting, a landscape, had both Cézanne and Van Gogh as its ancestors. Not terribly unusual, that. But the combination made a frighteningly unresolved work. There were violent streaks gnashing at the canvas, a canvas the ground of which held a quiet colorful landscape. What torture on that canvas. What suffering. Van Gogh had come to the eighties. Was this red circle on her own canvas giving the lie to her own quiet ground or was it there to make a formal statement the equivalent of the human one: there's no quiet without concomitant passion? Was that what the young painter was saying too? Why did it then seem so unresolved? Was her painting too unresolved? Was it her life too that was unresolved? Was she forcing her quiet on the new passion? Was this new form on her canvas a premonitory symbol? Was her relationship with Jim to end? Why couldn't she let what was be? Why was she always trying to be rational? Neither art nor life was rational. She knew that well. Whatever would be would be. Along with what was now would come the chance event. The miracle then of the momentary resolution. The momentary resolution like the ring of the telephone now.

"Hello, Nora." It was Jim's lilting voice. "What are you up to today?"

"It's not a special day, Jim. I'm beginning . . . to paint, of course. And you?"

"May I come over? Maybe you're right. Maybe I should forget Joyce, at least for a while. I'm getting bored with his aesthetic theory. Perhaps I should change the whole subject of my book. Like *Joyce and Modern Artists*–or more especially *Joyce and Nora.* I'd be ahead on that one, wouldn't I? I'd know Nora."

"Oh no, you wouldn't, Jim. I'm not like Joyce's Nora, or do you think I am?"

"Weell . . . shall I say Nora was compatible . . . marvelous . . . in bed?"

"Are you complimenting me, Jim?"

"Of course I am. Therefore I mustn't make comparisons. You are you, very special, very special to me, Nora. But can't I come over? Now?"

"But it's so early. I've hardly started. Haven't begun at all."

"I'll be over in twenty minutes."

There it was again. Again, being dictated to by a man. No private life really. No private work life even. Perhaps she should just be like the Duchamp bride in his *Large Glass.* Not visible. Permanently there. With the nine bachelors, also permanently there. The chocolate grinder. And it would be glass, glass, glass, broken only in parts, and quite accidentally. What a bride, that. But she'd have her privacy. Her work would be done. She would be all contained. The final bride, lifeless, transparent, dominating. She looked at her new canvas again. Should she paint out that red spot? Do away with its circle, make it an arrow or some sharp triangle–not the wholeness of the circle, the eternal movement of passionate earth. And the arrow or whatever would be black, or at the very least gray. Shape and form and color. Determinants all. Of her life. Of his life. Of all life. When she thought of all the space paraphernalia, those strange shapes based on eternal geometry, those sterile colors that would rise and penetrate the empyrean, she shuddered. Man-made and yet mysterious. Forms and shapes and colors of an overriding universe. Beckoning everyone to some realization of something never-ending. Something opaque and yet transparent. Something dead and yet alive. Matter, matter. Changing form.

"I'm coming," Nora exclaimed at the ringing of the doorbell. And there he was. Matter shape form eternity the *Large Glass* forgotten. In his arms. Red red red. She would leave the red circle in! When they separated still holding hands Jim was quick to notice the new canvas. "Nora, what is going on? You've hit the mark. What a dynamic canvas. And quiet too. So calm. You're changing." And as he looked, he held her close. "I like it. I like it. Are you happy with it too? You who are never happy with your work."

"I don't know yet. It's not finished. Do you really like it? But you do see something new, don't you?" She was pleased. Jim, despite his obsession with the nonvisual Joyce really had an intuitive sense of art.

"When I was in California, giving a talk at the California Institute of the Arts, on Joyce's aesthetics, I remember David Salle was a graduate student there. He seemed always to have a cigar in his mouth–and a mean face. I saw some of his work then. I liked it. Rather like Diebenkorn. But consider his work now. Changed, ugh. But your change, Nora–ah!"

"What a way to compliment me, Jim. So negative or circular or oblique. Why can't you be straightforward?"

"The bastardly touch of the academic. That's all. But really I don't want to be on a lecture platform. I hate it really. You know I'm essentially not a lecturer, just a curious frightened human animal who wants to know all."

"Frightened? You never seem frightened. What are you frightened of?"

"At the moment, Nora, of you. What you are doing to me. For example, why am I here when I should be at work? Why am I driven to be with you? I want to be with you too much, too much."

"Isn't that a negative compliment too? Why 'too much'? Is it love? Are you afraid of that? Of being in love? When you were with your wife before your hideous divorce (your word, you know) were you frightened too–of being too much in love?"

"I never loved Jane the way I love you, Nora."

"Oh, Jim, you've used the word. You've used the word *love*. For the first time to me. Are you using it hastily? Do you mean it, Jim? Are you using it to define your relationship to Jane? Is it only a matter of degree, then? You love me more than you loved Jane, but how do I know how much you loved Jane? It's a silly riddle. What was it like, that love?"

"Oh, it's stupid to compare. Maybe I should say simply, it wasn't love. Maybe it was just sex. What does it matter. It ended, and I am here, and Nora, shall we marry?"

The bride, the large glass, the nine bachelors, the chocolate grinding machine. Where were they now? In the Philadelphia Museum of Art. Nora now unrelated to them all. Just a simple woman being told by the man she loved he wanted to marry her. And she was happy! But was she? She suddenly burst into tears.

Jim took her in his arms, wiping away her tears. "What is wrong, Nora? Are you already married? Have you another lover? Or don't you love me at all? What is it?"

What is it, yes, what is it. Nora herself did not know. It was love. It was loss. It was ecstasy. It was sorrow. It was the beginning and the end. The random event that led to an inexorable resolution. It was not happiness. It was a yielding, a giving up of her own world. "Jim," Nora said, still sobbing. "I can't marry you."

"Why? What is it? Why can't you?"

"Hold me tight, Jim. Don't let me go, but I . . . I simply can't marry. It isn't that I can't marry *you,* don't you understand. It's that I simply can't marry."

"But that's madness, Nora. Why can't you marry?"

"Because I must remain whole. I can't give up a wholeness, can I? Don't you understand that when a man marries, he is still whole. He remains independent. But a woman, even today, doesn't remain herself. At least I know I couldn't. I'd immediately consider my own needs secondary. My studio would be secondary. My thoughts. I would be all yours. Just consider: here you are and we are not even married. I really didn't want to see you now. I am working. You interrupted me, but even now when I'm not married, without my approval, you came here. I had to receive you. Don't you understand? I don't know. I think it's all biological. Something about sperm and fallopian tubes and bonding and competition and maleness. Something about what an anthropologist friend of mine once said about wifeness, motherness. Women, he said, are the 'preservers of the egg of culture—its Temple Virgins.' How to be a woman, even a mother, and still remain myself, a painter, a person who—"

"Is that all, Nora?" Jim laughed as he pushed away the hair that had fallen over her face. "Is that all, my poor dear sweet Nora whose consciousness is ablaze. Don't you know I would never interfere with your professional life. Never."

"But you already have. Aren't you here, now, at eleven in the morning, when I should be working? Aren't you here now?"

"But if we were married, Nora, I would have seen you all night and in the morning. I wouldn't have to rush over here merely to be near you. Don't you understand?"

"No, it's not that easy. Yes, we would have been together all night, even had breakfast perhaps in the morning, but I still would be having some womanly responsibility toward you – like shopping for food for a dinner party for your colleagues or picking up your jacket at the cleaners or arranging for dental appointments or simply washing your clothes. Don't you see? You think now you would take over these things and some of my own chores. But as time would go on, you wouldn't. And then we'd want children. And then it would truly be the end of my career for a long time. How well I remember my own mother's frustrations. She was a sculptor, even had a show before she married, and then, why then it was over. My brother Dan came and I came – and out of her life went her art. It was only after we had left home that she got back to her work. But it wasn't easy. She still hasn't caught up. And basically it's not too different today."

"Oh, Nora, perhaps your mother just hasn't got the talent."

"You see, it's just your maleness that says that. As if women and men were equal. As if it didn't matter, that time didn't matter, that one could mature as an artist even as she breast-fed her babies. You simply don't understand. Why do you think even your Nora Joyce didn't marry until thirty years after they were living together? Of course she wasn't a professional woman. It was probably Joyce's idea anyway. And it was a different time. And, and anyway you simply don't understand. It's dreadful being a woman, but," Nora laughed, "quite wonderful too," she added as she brushed his lips with her fingers.

"Oh well. Let's not marry. We'll wait – thirty years – that's all," Jim said as he slowly unbuttoned Nora's blouse. And then they were making love and Nora was happy and sad. And she painted another canvas with a larger red circle and for many months on her canvases there wasn't a single black brushstroke, not a single stroke of gray.

At the Whitney: A Dialogue

NOT THREE, but two, she said. What would I do with three? Even three porcelain butter knives from China. Three is a triangle. I don't want another triangle. Are you in a triangle?

–Yes, I'm in an isosceles triangle.

–Oh, be reasonable. Are you married? Are you attached maritally or otherwise? Is the voice that is speaking to me now, has that voice spoken this very morning to some woman? Tell me.

–Yes, of course. At 11:15 to be precise. To Mary Lewitt, my secretary.

–Oh, so it is she whom you are involved with.

–Yes, very much involved. At the moment she is typing out the brief that is my pièce de résistance. I'll argue that one in front of the Supreme Court in October.

–No, no. You know very well what I mean. Is she secretary–and lover? Is she your lover too? That happens all the time in New York. As an exile from Nebraska I know. It's not just in the movies. It's right here, on Madison Avenue.

–Why are you so obsessed with the possibility of my being either married or being involved with some other woman. I'm here with you. It's Friday afternoon at the Whitney. Let's see, 2:10, no, 2:12 P.M. We are enjoying a lunch–a bit minuscule, but still a lunch, and you bug me with triangles of one sort or another.

–Because New York men are like that. That's all. First marriage, then the affair. During marriage of course. Then the next affair. An old serialism. Right?

–Yes, an old serialism. But not my kind. The only cereal I know is for breakfast. Have you ever had muesli? I started having that cereal in Geneva. You can find it here now in the States. Have you had it? Or don't you like cereals–only involved, are you, in serialism old or new? What about serialism in music? Do you like that? Anyway, what about simulation? Oh no. What about stimulation? Stimulation is better. Much better. Eroticism stimulation orgasm automobiles airplanes cells conduits spaceships, and Strategic Defense maneuvers. What about all those? Now tell me, what about those?

–All right. Let's forget the whole thing. No more triangles and certainly no more Star Wars. What's your case about? The one you'll be arguing at the Supreme Court. In Washington, I'm assuming.

–Yes, in Washington. The seat of the nation's power. No less. When were you last there? Want to come with me (not to hear me, of course) for the week then? What are you doing in October?

–The same thing I'm doing in July. Painting.

–But you'll be able to get away?

–Probably and not probably. But will you and I, will we, want to go away together in October? We can hardly manage a weekend without being uncomfortable.

–What do you mean "uncomfortable"? I'm never uncomfortable with you. What do you mean?

–You're so evasive, that is. You make me uncomfortable. Even in bed. You tell me things, things that–are not clear.

–Are not clear? In what sense not clear? You know how I feel about you?

–Do I? No, not really. Why do you think I'm worried about triangles? I'm uneasy. Yes, uneasy. I wish I could be sure you were really unattached. Single now with only a child or two a wife or two whom you have divorced but whom you have to support–not in the style to which they were accustomed. You see, I am thinking of your becoming "straitened," of living soon–with all the wives and children–in what you lawyers say, I am sure, are "straitened circumstances." But really it is the wife, isn't it, because of you men and divorces and women and relationships and triangles and obsessions, who really have to live with their children oppressed oppressed tearful in "straitened circumstances."

–There you go again. Now I'll say it directly: I am not married, never have been, and at the moment have only one, Christine Mansfield, whom I presently love.

–Oh, so you only "presently" love me. You see, you are already thinking of the next relationship. *Presently.* I don't know why I ever enter into relationships. Really. *Presently.* Then it's over. Then it begins. Then it's a triangle. Then it's a breakup. Then it's a new relationship. Then it's sad. In total it is simply depressing. I wish I weren't so damned biological. Primitive. Never foregoing the body. Never worrying about AIDS. Oh, maybe I should ask: Are you or have you ever been–a homosexual? Oh, forget it. Maybe I should become a Zen Buddhist. What about a deconstructionist–or is that passé. Would that help anyway. To rid me of my drives. To deconstruct ME? What do you think?

–Christine, what a depressing monologue. But don't you forget all threatening possibilities when you are in love?

–No, everything is so unpredictable. You say we should go away in October. What about July? Now. Where shall we go now?

–I can't now. I'm oppressed with work. Oppressed.

–You see. You can't go now. You say it's work. But where were you last night? Why didn't you call at 7:00 as you planned? Not at 11:30 when I was distraught with worrying about you? Why did you give me that phony excuse? How can I believe you? It could have been soap opera: *My mother came in unexpectedly.* Honest. Couldn't you make up a more interesting lie? Just look around you here, for instance. You could make up wonderful stories just out of these paintings. Something about suburban swimming pools. Dogs, torture on the city sidewalks, invasions of little men, ordeals at the Palladium, dancing incestuously in the nude.

–Would you like another coffee? How about some dessert? Strawberry shortcake. Very American. With a touch of the suburbs. Would you?

–Really, Frank. It's all so hopeless. So hopeless to talk to you. Let's go back to my studio. I won't even show you my new canvas. We'll just, just–go to bed.

–Yes, you and I and the bed. A triangle.

–Equilateral, Frank. Equilateral!

Green Caterpillar

IT'S A GREEN CATERPILLAR," he said. "Just look at it. It's a green caterpillar."

"Ridiculous." Jane winced at the description of her new station wagon. "It's hardly green and besides it's chunky. Not at all slithery and thin like a caterpillar. You have no sense of metaphor." She looked hard at Richard and wanted to cut off the wisp of hair, blond hair, that always fell into his left eye. She wanted to take the silver-rimmed glasses and throw them on the sand. She wanted to smudge his shirt–his starkly white shirt. She wanted to turn away, to leave the cottage near the ocean and walk away. She wanted to walk along the shore with bare feet. Alone. She wanted to catch the sound of the waves without looking at them but wanted them near, very nearby.

"Jane, the station wagon is green, and it looks like a caterpillar. And if you'd only get into it and drive to town maybe we could find something more interesting to argue about than the color and shape of your wagon."

Jane did not reply. Opened the door, placed her hand on the wheel (it was a high seat, and she would not confess to him that little as she was that was a disadvantage) as he quickly in one swift motion with his long legs sat down next to her slamming the door.

"Don't slam the door, for heaven's sake. You don't need to slam the door. It's a new car, you know. I want it to last."

"Wow!" was Richard's only response.

As Jane made three fast turns to the left–once to the left, twice, and then three times–each time swerving the right side of her body in a kind of rhythmic motion, she made a decision. She would not have Richard come back to the cottage. She would take him to the station. Would say good-by, thank-you. It was over. That was it. Over. No more of his stupid metaphors. His silly boyish exclamations. And his white shirts!

"Jane, you know that's a tree. Not a road, for heaven's sake. Look ahead, will you."

Jane ignored him and drove even more quickly as suddenly out of nowhere a truck headed in her direction. She was quicker than the driver and nimbly edged over to the side of the road quickly darting out again and regaining speed.

"What are you, a racing driver? Where'd you learn that art?"

Jane again ignored Richard and bit her lip. As she touched the lip with her right hand she felt an ooze. She knew it must be blood. It pleased her, that she could bite so hard, in the car, next to Richard. That blood would come.

Richard noticed her sly look in the mirror. "What'd you do? Great god, girl, you've blood on your lips. What'd you do that for?"

"For you. I did it for you."

"What do you mean, for me? You've bitten your lip for me? How come? Why?"

She looked at him. "To give you pleasure." She felt her smile slowly forming and held it there. She looked at him, lingering on his face.

"Look straight ahead, girl. Look at the road, not at me. Wow!"

She turned away and noted how the sand was becoming more rocky. They were getting closer to town. She liked that.

"Where are we going to eat? At Rotter's again? I hated the dinner last night."

"Yes, at Rotter's." A great idea. He hated the dinner.

"Hell. Let's try the new steak place. Tom tells me they have great steaks."

"No. I don't want steaks. We'll go to Rotter's."

"You're a rotter yourself. You know that. A rotter today. What's eating you."

"I don't like your shirt."

"This shirt? It's just an ordinary white shirt. What don't you like about it?"

"That's just it. It's just an ordinary white shirt."

"I'll be damned."

"Yes, you ought to be." They were silent for the next few minutes. Suddenly they heard a horn. "Wow! That's Mike and Mary. Wonder what they're doing going in that direction. They couldn't have eaten already. Maybe the Sterns are making the party after all. But they sure didn't invite us!"

"No, they didn't invite us." She was glad. She could say goodby quickly after dinner. Very quickly. He's really going to be surprised. She was relishing the pleasure of it right now.

"What are you smiling about?"

"I'm going to have a good experience. Soon. I'm anticipating."

"Ah, I like that, Jane."

"No, you won't, Richard. You won't. It's not what you think."

"What a mood. What a mood you're in today, Jane. I've always thought you moody. But today. Wow!"

She parked the car in the town lot. He was out ahead of her. Waiting near the entrance. "You couldn't wait for me, could you," she said. "Couldn't open the door for me."

"Hell, Jane. What's up? Since when do I open doors for you? It's a new wagon but I'm not a new man."

"You ought to be. Try it. You might begin by finding a good table while I go to the john." She left him at the door of the restaurant and very slowly as if she were walking in an academic procession she arrived at the door of the restroom. It was a wide door, a sliding door. Two black hinges on top. Obviously a handmade door. She pushed the door to the left, and then opened the ordinary door that said "Ladies." She looked at herself in the mirror. Her cheeks were flushed, and her black hair was disheveled. She looked at it. She rather liked the disheveled look. She would not comb her hair. Her lips were pale. She like that too. She would not put on lipstick. There was a bit of blood where she had bitten her lip. It was becoming hard. Coagulating. She would not wash it away. She liked the red swollen effect. She looked as if she didn't care. Didn't care. She looked as if she didn't know what she didn't care about. She dug into her little brown purse and found her eye pencil. She placed a little purple dot under her right eye. She liked the look of the red and purple. She was becoming dotted. Dotty Jane. She liked that. She washed her hands slowly, carefully, looking all the time in the mirror. She heard a knock. "I'm coming right out." She smiled at the high-heeled tall cool blond who was waiting as she walked out of the door. She had to slide open the first door. It was a good feeling. She slid it back in position as she retraced her steps toward the front of the restaurant looking for Richard who was seated at a table near the window. "A rotten table," she said sitting down.

"A rotten table at Rotter's. Why not?" He smiled.

She did not return the smile.

"Come on. Cheer up. You've already gotten a bloody lip. What more do you want?" He looked at her closely. "And what the hell is the purple spot under your right eye?"

"Don't you like it? I'm mixing colors. Making a palate of my face. You didn't like my last canvas. Did you. I'm obliging you. Making a new canvas with a new palate. Like it?"

He ignored her question. "I'm having lobster," he said looking at the menu.

"I'm having ratatouille. Wine. And a small salad. Coffee."

He ate the lobster well. Snipping, cutting, chewing. Never once looking at her. She touched her food lightly, slowly. Saying nothing. He almost smacked his lips as he wiped the napkin to the left to the right, left and right, when he finished. "That was good," he said. "Good. How was yours?"

"Good. Good." Now was the time. She was going to shock him. She relished the thought.

"What's playing at the mall," he asked. "I'd like a movie. You?"

"Not exactly."

"What do you mean 'not exactly'? Yes or no?"

"You won't be here to take me. That's all."

"I won't be here to take you? I am here, silly. Wow!"

"But you won't be any minute. I'm seeing you off to the station."

"To the station? Now? You idiot. It's only nine o'clock. Besides I'm staying for the weekend. Did you check on the movie? You don't like it, is that it?"

"No, I like it. I'm going as a matter of fact. It's *Breaker Morant.* I'm going to see it again. Alone."

"Alone? But I'm here. What's the matter? Are you serious? What do you mean you're taking me to the station? Jane, look at you. You sure do have a cold eye. Look how you are looking at me. Cold as a shark. Green too. You're looking green. A green caterpillar. You're a green caterpillar." He laughed. She laughed.

"Yes, I'm a green caterpillar. Caterpillars don't go to movies. They drive white shirts back to stations in green caterpillars otherwise known as station wagons. New ones."

They looked at each other. Richard's mouth really dropped. Almost to that white shirt. He stared at her. "You've got a green eye and a brown one," he said. "You've got a green eye and a brown one."

The train left at 9:45.

No Rabbits

She sat on the chair near the wooden basket. She was knitting. She worked the needles so quickly they flashed against the sun. She was sitting in the direct line of the sun. The French windows were wide open, and the cool water of the river lay below her. She never looked at the windows. Never saw the barges. Never noticed when a sailboat seemingly unoccupied slowly passed beyond her vision. He saw everything. He counted that within two hours there had been three barges, two sailboats. But even he ignored the numbers of cars, constantly driving driving near the water, on the road of the city, where sleek Porsches and old rusty barges never met but passed each other so near so far the times converging in the old and the new. She never looked. Only the wool seemed alive to her. To him she could only say, "Soon. Soon." Or at other times, her lips tight, with a slight sneer, she might say, "Yes. Yes." His fears grew with that kind of recognition to his questions. Her muted preoccupations. Her soundlessness. The knitting would last for hours. He always remained. Always remained. He longed to get up, to leave, to stretch his feet. Read Wittgenstein. His anxiety kept him there, glued to her chair, to the river, to the endless slow foamings of whitecaps and water. Today it was Sunday. He thought what a delight it would be to call up Tom to take a walk with him to their favorite bar, to try to unravel with him the strange circumlocutions, to decide again the relevance of the new and old Wittgenstein. But here he was, watching the unraveling of the skeins of wool: red, orange, black. And those fierce needles. Plying, plying the wool. Suddenly he felt tired. Absolute fatigue hit him, and he relaxed. Stopped his vigil. Relaxed. Allowed his eyes to close, his mind to wander.

The needles began to slow down. The skeins of wool took on less life. Colors were becoming neutral. Mary's eyes wandered to her husband's chair. Her sneer still hung on her lips. Hate hung there. She stopped knitting. She sat vacant for a moment, her hands on her lap, the skeins of wool quietly on the floor, and the needles falling gently on the rug. Her lips began to move. Suddenly more words than she had used for weeks were forming themselves. He was asleep. He did not hear. Did not hear her get up, stand near the window, look down. She remembered the Lawrence story, of a woman who accidentally fell out of a window, killing herself while hanging out her panties. She knew there were no accidents. Not of that kind. Not between a husband and a wife. Not when hatred was the connection with the world. She looked down. Nine stories were not too high. Nine or ninety though. To her the distance was years. Years of hatred. Her hatred was like a ball of wool. In her heart. But turned to stone. She could not move that stone. Hatred held her womb taut. She turned to her husband again. There he was. People called him handsome. At thirty-eight he had done well. A philosopher. But he could not bring her the philosopher's stone, only an ache, a torture. Her barren womb and her tortured heart. Both the same. And all he could think of was Wittgenstein. If he would only leave her alone. It was senseless her going to the hospital again. She would only return. To him. It was senseless merely to take pills. To knit, to sleep, to be watched over, not with love but with fear. Last time she had used a razor, and now below her was the river. The River Styx was all she wanted. She thought of a Cortázar story (what a reader she used to be!), of the young man who killed himself because he had the morbid talent of vomiting up a rabbit. After eleven small rabbits he could not stand it anymore. And he became a body splattered on the pavement, with the blood of all those rabbits surrounding him. Nothing would surround her on the pavement. Not even rabbits. She could not even vomit up a little live bunny. If he were to wake up, she would become transfixed again. She would begin to knit, to wind up her life in wool sweaters, diabolically. If he were to wake up, her hatred would make those needles flash.

Pure Will

"Birds do not sing in Cages."
—EZRA POUND

SHE SLEPT on the floor. It wasn't because she liked the coldness under her body or rejected the warmth of his bed. She slept on the floor as an act of pure will. Do this, do that, he always said. And she did this. She did that. Even in bed she did this, she did that. And then he would sleep. He didn't care. It was in November after a snowstorm when, leaving the bed after a long drawn-out night of lovemaking, at 4:00 A.M. She went to the window and watched how the flakes fell. They fell effortlessly. No force seemed to direct them in their falling. One by one, sometimes seeming thick as two by two, they fell to the ground; and though as she watched at first there was hardly what could be called even a spread of white, slowly, almost invisibly, the snow covered larger and larger areas, and always each flake could be seen separate, volitionless, falling here there near on top of other flakes to make finally a small mound that turned into a cover of white, through an effortless act of will. That is pure will, she thought, pure will, and I am lacking it.

As she turned away from the window of the bedroom that early morning and looked at her sleeping husband, she yearned to become the snowflake, volitionless, and yet pure will. She would lie on the floor, hug it in her own horizontal position, as if by denying a bed raised on four legs, she would be asserting herself in an act of pure will. She would be in a room with her husband and would sleep on the floor not to deny him but to become WILL.

Mary was up before her husband that November morning so

that it was only that night that he learned of her new resolution. "Cut the crap," was his response. "Get off that damn floor." It was then that he began to call her Mona Lisa because her only response to him was a smile.

She smiled through his curses that night, and since he was never one to use physical force, she found that her smile alone allowed her to retain her new bed of freedom, to achieve that harmony of pure will.

Her son gave her more trouble. Coming into the bed in the morning little Tom was bewildered to find only his father. Looking around and seeing his mother almost rigid on the floor he ran to her frightened that she was ill. She reassured him that she was fine, but when he wanted to lie down beside her she protested. She wanted to be the sole occupant of her new bed. Tom began to cry but Mary was adamant. She had gained a new strength. She got up to make Tom breakfast but he was not even to step on her spot of floor. "It is mine," she said. "My own."

Mary made Tom his breakfast that morning, and prepared her husband's coffee. When the baby cried, she went to her. Picking up the infant, kissing her, made her tremble. For the first time she felt a primeval physical womanly joy. "Little Annie," she kept repeating. "Little Annie."

"What about my eggs?" she heard Carl shout from the kitchen. "I'm coming, Carl," she shouted back to her husband, and when she entered the kitchen, she walked up to him, kissed him happily on his lips and smiled. He frowned in response. "What about my eggs?" he said slowly again. And she thought of the snowflakes and a line of Pound came into her head: "What whiteness will you add to this whiteness, what candor?" Mary knew she would not find candor in Carl, and the whiteness was her whiteness, her act of pure will. She turned to the pot of coffee and watched the feathery trail of luminous white steam. She had allowed the coffee to boil.

Nun's Story

To hold a nun on your thumb is not easy. Just try it. Her habit slides down and tickles. John Feeble, I must say, likes the sensation. I do not. That tickle is a mickle much. It gives me no pleasure, but reminds me that the tickle is the tickle of a nun. Incomplete coition. But John likes that kind of thing. Each to his own, etc. I for one like to carry the nun around for a day and put her down. I can stand the tickle for a day, no longer. When I put her down she leaves. She comes back the next day and never tells me where she's been. Does she sleep, eat, go to a nunnery? She never tells me. Come to think of it. She never talks. Has she a voice? Unlikely. Probably her tongue has been removed. By the bishop. One day I saw him walking down the road holding a staff. The tip of the cane was covered with blood. And dangling down from it was something that looked like a piece of flesh. Round at the bottom, long on its sides, and cut straight across. Like a tongue. No doubt the tongue of my nun. John Feeble said he once heard her name. I say she has no name. He couldn't tell it to me anyway. And he has imagination. Rotten thing to have. He has nightmares. I don't. I cut those things short. You can always nip a nightmare in the bud. It's a matter of control. John Feeble has no control. He goes on and on about nuns and names. Even about bishops. No, about that one bishop with the staff and the blood and the dangling tongue. Once, he told me, he talked to the bishop. He said he had a name, too. I said of course bishops have names. Yes, said he. The bishop's name is Reilly. Bishop Reilly. And a good name too, I said. Bishop Reilly. I once went to school with a kid named Bill Reilly. Come to think of it he could be the bishop. Naw, I guess not. Bill Reilly couldn't even count his rosary. Bishops have to have some kind of brain. Bill had none. But he could run faster than anyone in the class. Beat me. Always. And I'm a pretty good runner. Ask the nun. I give her a run for her thumb ride. Whoosh, I say, and I dart out of the flophouse, race straight up East Broadway, and back in fifteen minutes two seconds. I know she's real proud of me. She comes back, doesn't she. Each day. Of course I don't always give her the ride. Sometimes I just sit and watch her. She has a funny habit you know. I mean, you know, the thing she wears. It's gray. Gray all over. I think the pockets are inside. Under all that gray material. Sometimes I wonder. Is she scratching or what when suddenly in goes her hand, under her habit, and whoo there's a zinging sound. It lasts about three minutes. I like that. Then out comes her hand and the habit tickles again. That I don't like, as I told you. John Feeble likes that a lot. But he hates it when her hand goes in and out. He hates the zinging. No telling about taste. I often wonder about that too. Taste. Why? Why the difference. OK, childhood and all that. Listen, I know Freud too. Don't be such a wise guy. You don't even have a nun. So shut up. Listen to me. Taste. Why? Take the nun. She has another habit. You know. The habit. The thing she wears. It is never dirty. But it smells. You're darn right. Stinks. How do I know of what? But I'm talking about taste. She has taste: she wants a clean habit. But it stinks. What kind of taste is that? Of course I hate the smell. No, shut up. It's not sweet woman smell. What do you think I am? Of course I'd fuck a nun. But not my nun. Sometimes I wonder who the hell you are and what the hell you think I am. Incestuous or something. She's my nun, I tell you. Oh cut it out. She's not for hire. And anyway how do I know she has a cunt. Of course she's a woman. But how come, I mean. How come all day she doesn't pee or something. I mean it. All day long on my thumb and she doesn't pee. Don't give me all that stuff. It's in the cunt, isn't it. Around it or something. Nuns pee, don't they. Once my sister watched a nun do it.

She really did. All that rustling of skirts and things. But she really did do it, my sister said. Of course nowadays they more or less look normal. No long habits, etc. But my nun has a habit and doesn't pee. I guess it's just a matter of free will. You can control it after all. Once I didn't pee a whole day. A whole day. Mind over matter. I didn't pee a whole day. And I'm as strong as an ox. No stones in my kidney or anything. Listen, did you ever have an X-ray of your kidney. Terrible. Put iodine or something inside you. God-awful. I imagine if you're a woman with a cunt it's different. Not so painful. How the hell do I know why they gave it to me? No, that was in that old flophouse when a young doctor decided to do some charity work. Naturally I was his first patient. Charity, you know. No, that wasn't the day I didn't pee. How would he know anyway. There's always the stink in the place. On me? You kidding? Just look at my pants. Only a smudge of yellow. Right? No, I'm not like my nun. But I don't stink. Only on Sundays. When John Feeble comes with some of his muscatel. Of course I hold the nun when I drink. Don't forget she comes on Sundays too. Every day I told you. Naw, she doesn't mind the wine. Never asks for any though. I told you she doesn't talk. But did I tell you she opens and shuts her lips? That's a drag. It sounds like a smack but it's downright dirty. A nun smacking her lips. I told you I never could understand taste and all. No taste. OK, no manners. Poor upbringing. For all I know the bishop was her father. He must've had no upbringing. Walking around with a tongue on a staff. No upbringing. And John Feeble says when you come right down to it it's all a matter of upbringing. And I tell you that's about the only thing I agree with John Feeble about. Upbringing. Now, don't get me wrong. That guy has none. Absolutely no upbringing. But he knows about it. See? Simply knows that upbringing is important. Says the nun has none. Get what I mean. N-o-n-e. And he says I have plenty. Plenty. You see it too, don't you. You know you're not a bad guy after all. If you want to come around next Sunday night I'll let you see the nun get off my thumb. Aw, don't thank me. Just my upbringing. Upbringing. That's all.

Disciple

YOU ARE GETTING READY. I sense it in the movement of your left arm. Raise it a little and you will feel the readiness yourself. No, not so slowly. Oh, not so quickly. Gently, gently. Yes, that's right. Gently. Don't you feel it?

–No, I don't.

–Don't you feel it? Well, then, try again. Try again.

–I can't. The arm is stiff, maybe paralyzed. Who knows. Anyway, stiff.

–But you just did it. How could it be so stiff so soon? Try it again. Lift the hand first maybe, holding your fist tight. Give yourself some leverage. Some pressure. That's it. Only the fist of your left arm, please. Gently now raise the whole arm and let the fist relax. Good. Now you've done it again. Good. OK, are you ready now?

–Yes, now.

–Let your arm remain there, yes, high up, higher. OK, now bend your knees and lift your whole body up up, again gently. Fine. You're doing it right. Fine. Higher higher. Now do you hear me? Throw out both arms and pretend you're swimming a crawl stroke. Yes, that's it. Fine. Now don't think. Never think up there–and FLY. You've got it. Hurrah. How does it feel? Do you hear me? Karl, do you hear me up there? Karl, Karl, where are you now? Don't disappear. Don't stay up there more than a minute. Karl, where are you? Come down, Karl. Come down, Karl. Do you hear me?

David looks at his watch. He'll time him. Seven minutes past ten. No clouds in the sky. Eight minutes past ten. *Karl, where are you?* David takes out his telescope. Peers hard. Blankness only. Is the lens defective? No. No. Thirteen minutes past ten. There's a speck appearing. Some small speck. What is it? Not Karl. The speck is growing. Growing into a bloody red. The sun? Of course not. I'd be blinded by it. The red circle is growing larger. It's beginning to have shape. My god, I see arms, legs, a head. A red leering head.

–Hey, Karl, is it you? What are you leering at? Me? Come off it, Karl. And come down, this minute. This minute.

The arms are disappearing! And the legs. The red is fading. The shape is breaking up. But the leer is still there.

–Karl, where are you, you Cheshire cat. You've betrayed me. COME DOWN.

Graven Image

He did not like it. He simply couldn't handle it. The door seemed to collapse as soon as he placed the hammer near it. To use a nail, therefore, was useless. He sat on the log and looked hard at what was almost a Daliesque door–soft, shapeless, ready to fall toward its own center. Inclined to the right, the door sagged, almost wept, in its hinges. Now more than ever its dried-up, peeling redwood matched the timber of the cottage. The door was more than his own present. It was past and goddammit future too. It looked like his own sagging days–desiccated, broken down, unremittingly peeling. Yet his business was not to think but to do. To get the thing fixed. To have a place to enter, a place to go into and out of, a place to remain in–closed, enclosed. Secure within walls. In a woods, away from noise, telephones, people–and wives. Even his children seemed to be bodies to get away from. Even little Nina, with the curls and the smile that made him weak with happiness. If he had to be away from her to get that sense of enclosure, well, he just had to be. It was all in the plan. To be alone, to work with his hands, to carve that wood into the image that had been tormenting him long before he gave up his teaching job to discover what was that ache in his head that defied X-rays and doctors and turned him to psychiatrists and then away from them with the sense that the ache must be the image that had to be carved: the *idée fixe* that was no longer symbol but a reality craving to be born. He suddenly felt a strange sympathy toward Nora, his first wife, whose pregnancy had maddened him because she seemed so happy with it. Wasn't he now happy with his hands and his head swollen with the ache that was the image, that thing to be realized, to be born? This is what it must be like to be with child, to feel that stir within that means full being, the breath of life, the slight purr of consciousness–a minute before unrealized, soon to be born, to be alive. Sentient. A thing to endure. As he must endure to make it endure. Endure as that door will not. Perhaps the best thing would be to eliminate it entirely, to let the thing cave in–or simply to tear the thing down and first to make the door instead of the image so that the image would have the space, the enclosed space, to be born into. Without the place to go in and out of the image itself would have no roots, and the ache in his head would go on. And that he could not endure.

He picked up the hammer again and almost felt the door cringe as he approached. It was an easy target. Dismantling the door would be almost too easy, though it also meant replacement, the harder task. He would learn, he felt, that to make is cruel, because it requires the will to destroy. The door would be his first foray into the creative act. He felt that ache in his head again, and his hands began to shake. He held the hammer as steadily as he could and struck hard. The one blow was sufficient. Amazingly hundreds of pieces of wood scattered inside the cottage and out. A snowfall of wood–splinters, segments large and small, in a kind of arpeggio of discrete pleasures of sound. So sound wasn't that bad after all. If it came from wood, and things fell apart, with only himself to hear it.

He knew he would have to make the new door quickly. Knew too he was a fool to have broken the old one without first having made the replacement. But there were no mosquitoes this time of year, and though an occasional raccoon might wander his way, he was pretty certain it would leave him and his cottage alone: he was the stranger, the indecent human animal, unpalatable to the gentle raccoon. And no birds would enter. Birds want to fly.

He would have to find the right size lumber for the door. He walked over to the small shed near the piled-up firelogs. Though that door seemed stuck to its hinges, with a few hard pushes with his body he forced it open. He hadn't been in the shed for a whole year, in fact since last September when he had taken out the beaten old couch from the cottage and placed it in the shed for storage. As he looked around the small area he was taken aback to see a freshly stained redwood door, hinges and all, exactly the size of the one he had so mercilessly torn down. He was rather appalled in fact to see it. What demon or angel or more likely what man or woman had placed it there? Was he not going to be alone? Was he to be dogged by some overseeing presence? Was he to be cared for again, here in the New Hampshire woods where he had come to be alone? Crazy of him to think of some human interference in his life here. Probably he had just not seen the door last year when he had put the couch there. But it was a bit uncanny. Need so quickly filled was almost demonic. Reality was not usually that kind. Perhaps, however, his eye had failed him. Perhaps the door was not an exact replica of the old one. He took out the tape measure from his pocket and carefully measured length and width, walked quickly to the cottage and measured the door frame. He almost wished the door would not fit. But it did. He couldn't afford to think that the door had not been in the shed all along. This was no time for uncertainties, no time for mysterious presences.

He again went into the shed and found a sander. Sanding along the door jambs he began to get that exhilarating feeling he used to have when he went trout fishing with his father. He remembered the feeling never had lasted long. His father's good temper was brief. He never knew when some slight movement on his part would enrage his father and he would lose the camaraderie he had longed for. A relationship with his moody father was only a dream. That was an ache too that he carried with him. But it was easier through the years to carry that ache than the ache in his head. The ache in his head was a sign of the failure (and possible fulfillment?) of his adulthood. That childhood heartache though painful had at least been appeased through his relationships with older men during the war, the horrid Vietnam War that taught him vicious politics as well as love.

He thought the door frame was now ready for its new occupant. As he walked back again to the shed he became suspicious of himself: had he really seen that new door? Was it a mirage of his own despair, of his great need for a new beginning? Was it a mirage like that time during the war when he was sure he had seen a floating baby with seared flesh rising out of the rice patch? He surely had better control of himself now. After all he was no longer giving commands to demolish whatever was in sight. He was alone now. He hadn't killed anyone today–he had only demolished an old broken-down door.

She stood there in the doorway of the shed. Wearing old jeans, a thin cotton top covered by a light green army jacket, the kind worn by the men as camouflage during the war. That jacket had always seemed to him high camp: its decorative designs not trees and rocks but strange insignia of the unconscious, phallic symbols of war-weary men. She was smoking a cigarette. Her long blond hair slightly pushed back over her left ear as if by wind but more likely by her unpolished fingernails. She watched him coming toward her and noticed his right eyebrow raised in controlled surprise.

"Who are you," she heard him say. She smiled, not answering, as she waited for him to approach.

"Where in the hell have you come from?" For reply she extended her hand. He was surprised to find himself taking it, even holding it a bit too long.

"I hope you like the door," she said.

So that was it. Another human being to dislodge him from himself, to protect him from privacy and the ache in his head. He could hardly control the rage that was building up in him. "Wh-what do you mean?" he asked. "How did you know that I was going to take down that door? When did you get into the shed?

How did you manage to bring up the door in the first place?" He thought of Karen, his new wife. This girl must be one of her tricks. Or was she just a trick of his eye, a satisfaction of a longing he thought himself in control of?

This time she laughed. "I know you," she said. "You have needs. Chiefly of doors, but only doors made of redwood, with hinges easily placed–and above all of hinges that do not squeak."

He looked at her closely now, his rage easing and a terrible physical curiosity gnawing at him. "All right," he said. "If you brought the door, you'll have to pay for it."

"But I thought you'd be grateful," she said. "I hardly thought you'd be thinking of some kind of punishment. I bore you this gift. Why don't you thank me, simply be grateful?"

"You bore a gift that I needed, but you brought yourself," he said. "You have come uninvited. I can't bear to have anyone around now. If you knew I needed a door, didn't you also know that I wanted privacy to . . . to create?"

"Create? But you don't know how," she said.

"Don't know how," he cried out. "How dare you say that to me? You'll have to pay for those words too," he said as he grabbed her hand, turned her around and pushed her into the shed. He then closed the door but with such force that the spring behind it broke loose and made a high piercing sound as it fell to the ground. The sound made him turn toward the door. As he did so he thought he saw it open slightly and a form slip through. Turning back to the shed he wanted to ask the girl whether she too had seen the fleeing form.

He began to speak but stopped short. The girl was no longer there. He began to tremble. "Where are you?" he managed to say in a weak voice. There was no reply. He turned again toward the door and rushed out, hoping to catch sight of her or even of the fleeing form. He ran about ten yards and stopped. There in front of a huge boulder, a landmark of the property he had purchased five years ago, was the green jacket but lying as if it had been there for months–rumpled, muddied, and even with the stench of mildew. He picked up the jacket wildly and ran back into the shed hoping to see the girl again. But she was not there. Suddenly he thought of the new door. It too was gone. Instead of the door, in the very spot that he thought he had left it, a new but longer spring lay, made of shining new metal. It seemed to gleam at him, to smile at him contemptuously. He bent down to pick it up, sweat on his forehead and on his palms. He touched it gingerly, expecting it to snap back at him, growl or explain the absence of the girl. But it felt like a spring, a spring of shining new metal. He dropped it to the floor again, and again heard that high piercing sound as it fell to the ground. The sound made him again turn toward the door. He expected nothing there. And nothing was there. He thought the sound had lasted longer than the first time but he knew now not to believe his own senses, eyes or ears. The sound too may have come from some new malfunction of his mind.

He could not bear the shed. He moved almost in a trance to the door and toward the cottage. He was afraid to approach the cottage but yet he knew that if he could get back to the cottage he might regain control of himself, at least to the extent of remembering whether or not he actually had encountered a strange woman on his property, property that he had purchased only because it was uninhabited for at least twenty miles in any direction. No one could approach the place who had not the benefit of his own map. How did this woman manage to get here? But worse yet how did she manage to escape? Remembering that he would not have a door this night and feeling the cooler air of approaching evening, he became chilled and longed for a hot cup of coffee. He would make himself a cup. Perhaps that would help to place things in perspective. As he stood in the door frame, he felt faint with fear: there before him stood the girl. Her jacket off, coolly confronting him, she asked: "But what was the punishment you were thinking of?"

He could barely speak through fear and bewilderment. "How did you get back here?" he managed to ask.

Again her only reply was a smile as she extended her hand. Again he held it, almost clinging to it in a panic that was making him nauseous. Suddenly he felt himself beginning to faint. When he opened his eyes, he was lying nude on what he recognized as the old couch in his shed, but he did not remember the quilt covering him. It looked like an old American patchwork quilt that he recalled he had seen in his grandmother's home in Vermont: the patches were of black velvet, some finely handpainted with designs of poppy and dogwood sewn with silken threads.

He looked for the girl, but again she had escaped. My god, he thought, I must be going mad. His whole body began to tremble uncontrollably.

"The coffee will be ready in a moment," a voice was saying as he searched the room for the body of that voice only to discover that he was no longer in the shed but in the cottage in his own bed.

"Or do you think hot tea would be better for you now," the same voice continued.

"Where are you," he heard himself say in a voice that he did not recognize.

"Where else, silly," he heard. "Making a pot of tea for you, of course."

He turned his eyes in the direction of the stove and there she was, smiling as she competently fixed him some tea.

"Where have you been?" he asked, his voice crazily pitched because of his rising frenzy.

"I thought you'd like to begin your punishment now," she said calmly as she walked over to him with the tea. "Have your tea and then it can begin," she said as she kissed him on the forehead and then began to undress with the kind of teasing expertise that his new wife always managed even when she knew he hated her most. His rage at those times destroyed him even as it created her passion for him. God, what a neurotic relationship it is, he found himself thinking even as he watched the girl undress and felt his panic ease and his desire for the stranger become almost unbearable.

"Well, here we are at last," she said. "But do drink your tea first, dear, or your punishment might be a bit chill."

Tea seemed to be the last thing he needed but in his fear that she would again escape him he drank the hot tea quickly, even though it burned his tongue and throat.

"How did you know I wanted to punish you in bed?" he asked as he placed the cup on the night table and without gallantry hastily fell upon her.

It was over in a few minutes. He closed his eyes with pleasure as he lay back on the pillow beside her. His sleep was more peaceful than it had been in a long time. When he opened his eyes again it was pitch dark. As he tried to reach for the light he felt terribly itchy. He seemed to be wearing something unfamiliar. Whatever was itching him certainly came from something he was wearing. The feel of it was unfamiliar. Turning on the light he discovered he was wearing the camouflage jacket. He then remembered the girl. She was not in the bed. He looked wildly through the small cottage. She was nowhere to be found. He thought of the shed, and uncomfortable as he was in the jacket he ran toward the door frame only to be hit by something hard. In the frame was the new redwood door, carefully positioned, firmly placed. Dazed, he stumbled back to bed. Suddenly the ache in his head was unbearable. "Dammit," he shrieked. "I can create. I have created an image in my head. I have possessed it in my body and have closed it and sealed it in a door."

"And we are home at last," the stranger said, as she kissed him on the head.

Lover

SHE DECIDED. He was the other. Not the lover. The lover would talk to her in her own tongue. Speak to her with the music of her own words. Touch her with the rhythms of her own body. He would not be the other, but the lover. The lover was not the other. The other was alien. His face a map of rude continents. His smells belonged to other animals. Not human. His touch, not warm, soothing, casual. No. His touch was stinging. Like a sudden electrical impulse. A cold shock of water. Not of rain. No. Rain was familiar. Rain was from the lover, not from the other. She put her face toward the sky. Not even a drop of rain. No lover.

She was a child when it began. She played with blocks. She stung her toe. She turned the other cheek when the sullen boy hit her. She did not cry. She knew he was the other, not the lover.

She was betrayed. Not by the lover, by the other. The lover tried to reach her. Through the windowpane. He could not break it. He touched the glass with his lips. She placed her lips on the opposite side. Opposite each other. Opposites together. She and the lover. He was not the other.

The train stopped. It was a long station. Between the waters and the mountain. She looked out the window. She saw the other: scraggly beard, one eye, arm in sling, pipe in mouth. He signaled to her. He was the other. Not the lover. His stench circled the train. She saw its emanation. Saw it. A thick yellow mass, covering the tracks. She closed her eyes. She choked on the scrofulous air that did not come from the lover.

She reached for her coat. It was black. Worn. Worn thin from long wearing. She was cold. She hugged it to her body as she walked. On Forty-second Street. New York. The city. A man swayed back and forth. His pockets bulged: bottles, rags, three bent keys dangling. He came close to her. "Are you . . ." she stammered. She drew back. She saw his bloodshot eyes. You are not the lover. You are the other.

He touched her left breast. Kneaded it. She looked down. Black, blue, new colors on her left breast. He looked. He marveled. She smiled. *You are the lover. You have transformed my body.*

"You are six years old," the teacher said. "Why do you clutch your desk at the corners? Why do you do that? Why?" She looked down at her hands. They were clenched. She had closed them so tight they hurt. She could not relax them. Why? She looked at the board trying to read. She spelled out five letters: O-T-H-E-R.

She ate the carrot. A sweet carrot. Who had cut off the green stem? Who had washed the clean soil from this bright orange carrot? She bit the carrot. The noise was loud. Familiar. She looked out the window. Into the garden. He was gathering more carrots. Four eyes met. He was the lover.

It was outdated. The language. Too many words. Each word an embellishment. Lushness disguised the meaning. She could not decipher the code. It came from the other. Not from the lover.

"A voice comes to one in the dark. Imagine." Beckett writing. The voice is the signal. The signal of the lover.

She approached the room. The dining room. The table was set. One setting. For the other. She retraced her steps. She walked out the door. The back door. Down the street. Toward the lover.

He reached the stair. Was standing there. At the landing. He did not ascend. She did not know: was he the other or the lover?

She sat at the typewriter. The words came. Nonsense words? *Lichen. Stone. Bedrock. Beside. River. Mountain. Home. Home?* The words were from the lover.

The bell rang. She ran down the stairs. At the door a green coat, green hat, green shirt, green tie, green pants, green suitcase. His green pipe was moving up and down in his mouth. "What are you saying?" she shouted. He took the pipe out of his mouth, spelled out the word: O-T-H-E-R. She stepped backward. He leered. He was not the lover.

She raised the hood of the car. A knocking sound hurt her ears. The engine? The muffler? No shock absorbers? Her eyes looked at the dirt, the grease. She saw his arm. In a sling. She smelled his odor. He was not the lover.

She turned the knob. Of the rococo door. Reliefs. John. Paul. The desert. She could not enter. Not through the door. The reliefs held her. He was behind the door. The lover. He did not greet her. He received her stare.

She lay flat. On her back. The shades drawn. It was four o'clock. In the morning. A bit of light near the sills. Just a bit. On one sill a stone. On a second a book. The book was green. It was the other's.

She walked in the garden. Near the tree. The two cardinals pursued each other. She watched the red. She watched the brown. She saw them fly. Their pursuit. Lovers.

Near the roses. The rose bushes. Only a single rose. She touched the petals. She bent down. The light fragrance soothed her. Until she turned. Saw the snapping turtle. In the shell. She walked near it. It opened its mouth. Its pink baby mouth. She picked it up by the tail. Held it. Saw its lively eyes. Staring at her. Saw its phallic body extending. She put it down. The mouth opened. She placed a stick in it. Snap went the mouth. It was the other.

This is the attic. This is the stair. This is the cellar. These are the doors. This is the stove. This is the table. This is the fireplace. This is the bed. He is not here. Neither other nor lover. But who is the shadow near the tulip tree? It is the lover.

She tasted the soup. She tasted the roast. The potato, the spinach, the peas. She ate all the salad. She cut through the melon. Drank all the tea. She looked at the tea leaves. There were three:

one for the lover, one for the other. She could not say "one for me."

There was the green room, the blue room, and the pink. She looked into all three. Only the shadows moved. In the green, the other; in the blue, the lover; and in the pink, her shadow. Quivering.

In the mansion a huge ballroom. An orchestra playing. Gowns and tuxedos. Soft sounds of speech, of laughter, of feet moving. She was dancing. In the center. Her white gown was gossamer. She smiled at her partner. Was he lover or other? He had touched her bare arm. He had kissed behind her ear. He had removed her gleaming pearls. He had touched her shoulder. They were dancing and gliding. They had the whole floor. She opened her eyes. A green jacket on the floor.

In the garden. Again. A fountain. She turned her head. In the direction of the sun. A shadow in front of her. Tree behind. She walked toward the fountain. Toward its spray. Brushing away drops of water from her face, she looked into the basin. At that mirror. At her face in the mirror. At the face behind the mirror. Peering at her. At the slant of the sun. The length of the tree. At the shadow behind that tree. At the shadows behind that tree. The moving shadows behind that tree. At the tree.

"I Am Not I Any Longer When I See"

—GERTRUDE STEIN

"BUT I WANT TO KNOW what it is like," Veronica insisted.

"What is what like," John asked.

"You know very well what I mean. What is it like after you have seen me, made love, spent hours and hours with me. What is it like to return home to June? What do you say to her? What is it like?"

"Are you trying to ask how do I hide my guilt—or my happiness?"

Veronica loved that smile. When John said *happiness* it became physical, like the visible glow after lovemaking. She felt even now in her anxious query that impossible sweet desire making her shudder. "Both," she said, "guilt and happiness."

"Well, I drive the car up the driveway, may or may not put it in the garage (depending on how controlled I am)," John added still smiling, "and then walk up the steps to the entrance. Turn the key, and walk in. That's it. Simple, isn't it."

"No, I mean when you suddenly face June—what do you say? Do you kiss her? Do you merely say hello? What do you say? What do you do?"

"Oh, Veronica, why do you ask? You mustn't try to imagine me in my own home. I am here. I am with you. Isn't it enough that I suffer, that I have pain when I leave you?"

"But you've told me you like June, even love her. Why is it pain? It's not pain; it's guilt. And you can't stand it. You are already thinking it's impossible. Two women whom you love. I can read it. I can read it on your face. Do you know you've become all gray in the years you have known me? Oh god, you are ending it. I know. Each gray hair is the beginning of the end. The hair delivers the prophecy. You'll always have your June."

"Why do you say all this? Are you trying hard to end it? Let's not begin this all over again. I am here. You are here. We've had a lovely day, and as a matter of fact, I have to go, as you well know. It's late." John looked at his watch as he lay beside her and then in that repressed controlled way he had to avoid a discourteous speedy good-by he sat up and announced he was taking a shower.

Veronica lay quietly, let her disheveled hair embroider the pillow and waited. She listened to the pelting of the water on the tub and imagined his movements in the shower. That long body, those sensitive hands covering with soap his stomach, his back, his legs, his arms, his cock–that lather with which he had so often covered her own body. She listened, waiting for his return.

Soon John was walking into the bedroom searching for his clothes–pants, underclothes on the floor, shirt hanging on the back of the chair. He looked at her smiling not talking ignoring what he must have seen on her face–that blankness that was neither terror nor pain, a face drained of all emotion. Fully clothed, obviously more cheerful because he was leaving, because he would not be late for dinner with June and his children. He walked up to the bed, tousled Veronica's hair and kissed her on the lips. "I'll call," he said, expecting no response. He was gone.

She lay there. Time seemed of no consequence. She was of no consequence. John was of no consequence. Perhaps it was half an hour, an hour. When she stirred, she saw through her window the sun lowering behind the trees. She watched it slowly disappear. It seemed to her that she was moving with the sun. Suddenly, when the sun had thoroughly disappeared from her sight, she felt a surge of strength. Her body completely awakened. She leaped up, showered, got dressed. She wanted to go to her typewriter and write. Something had snapped or something had been torn from her, and in its place something had been born. What was it? But it wasn't a thing, an object. It was a feeling, like love. A new love had entered her. It was a love for the sun that had disappeared. A love for the emerging darkness in the sky. A love for her table, her paper, her pens, her typewriter. A love for her own bedroom, her own kitchen–stove, table, chairs, pots, pans, dishes, silverware. Things she alone had selected. Her own words on paper. Her paper. She walked slowly through her apartment, looked at her paintings as if they were newly hung. Looked at her couch hugging the wall, her piano with a page of Mozart opened, a pencil nearby. She looked at the piano stool with its black cushion, at her cocktail table piled high with art catalogues, invitations to recent shows. She looked and felt joy.

She looked again at her paintings on the wall, looked particularly at a painting of childlike trees, an irregular path leading to a toy house that the artist Stamos had made on the occasion of her marriage: there was the heart, the wobbly calligraphy of I LOVE YOU YOU LOVE ME inside that red drawing of a heart with initials childishly inscribed and she suddenly knew what Gertrude Stein had meant when she wrote: I AM NOT I ANY LONGER WHEN I SEE. Yes, she was no longer the Veronica whose identity depended on John's love. She need no longer say I AM I BECAUSE MY LITTLE DOG KNOWS ME.

She walked quickly to the closet to get her coat. She must take a walk, look at Fifth Avenue with her new eyes, her new body. When she opened the closet door to reach for her coat she saw on the floor a pair of John's sneakers kept there for their tennis games. She stared at them as if they were strange, inappropriate, alien objects. She stooped to pick one up, held it close to her, touched its white leather, smelled its strong sweet odor, looked at the shoelaces gnarled and dirty, and slowly put the sneaker down. She closed the door, leaned against it, that door that John had painted red as a sign of their passion! Her chest heaved with her sobs. It was useless, useless. I AM I BECAUSE JOHN LOVES ME. I AM I BECAUSE JOHN LOVES ME, she repeated. Her shoulders shook as she walked sobbing to her bed and threw herself upon it. It was her coat that lay upon the floor.

Lost

LET US BE CONTENT, she said, and run off the letter to Jane. It will be either a reminder or an invitation or a thank-you note, a bread-and-butter letter, an encomium, or a letter of regret. It will be words and words are containers and on a letterhead and in an envelope it will be contained. Jane loves words and words are Jane's, and she will be happy to receive it to read it to hold it to place it in her folder to return to it to reread it and after a long pass to answer it with her words that are different from yours, she said, and so let us begin the letter right now. But I have no paper, I said, paper with my name on it, that is, I said. I have pads with no lines on them, will that do, I said. And of course, she said, and off she went to get the typewriter, and sat down and took the sheet of paper, torn from the pad, and placed it in the typewriter and smiled at me and said, now what will it be: a reminder an invitation a thank-you note or a letter of regret. None of those, I said, none of those just a letter, a gossipy wonderful letter telling her about you and me, I said. But what of you and me, she said, what gossip of you and me, she said that Jane doesn't know, that she would want to hear about just now, she said. About last night, I said, last night, I said, when the dog left the room and ran right out down the hall toward the elevator waited for it to stop walked in with two other people indifferent people walked out of the lobby out of the door into the street onto the road and ran past the traffic light down two blocks to the right one to the left and right down into the subway and then was lost lost and here you are and here I am writing to Jane without a dog just his leash with his food with that nice warm wooly jacket that we bought in that strange store in SoHo last May when Jane was in Venice and her studio was robbed and she came back with fifty photographs and two huge new canvases that she sold to that rich collector and never minded about her robbery and was ever so content. Let us be content, you said, and that is what I want to be, I said, as I wiped my eyes with the Kleenex from the pink box and thought of cans and cans of dog food and the warm wooly jacket sitting on the bedroom floor with its dog odor and dog fur and dog dog dog . . . .

Uptight

IT ALWAYS HAPPENS on the way to the supermarket. There is the little girl jumping rope and the boy on the bicycle holding it steady, leaning forward, one foot on the sidewalk, talking to his friend. She is uneasy clutching her Greek handbag walking toward the supermarket from the parking lot.

He's always there waiting for her. But she has to shop, at least once a week. In this small town, with only one market, how can she avoid him? Does she, does she, want to see him? To look at him with his baggy trousers, his unlighted cigarette dangling from his mouth, his thin, unjacketed arms, with a worn Norwegian black and white sweater?

Sometimes he lets the cigarette move up and down as he smiles at her. His smile is worse than his stare. He seems not to be able to manage his mouth. Not because of the cigarette. It's the thinness of those lips. A kind of misplaced hairline. Often she pretends not to see him. She opens her bag, looks as if frantically in need of a handkerchief, keys, or money, pretends to find the object, snaps the bag shut at the very moment that she is two steps beyond his stare. Somehow she feels him turn, feels those piercing eyes through her tan raincoat. But she's safe. Passed him. He's never followed her. She feels secure.

Today, she nears the entrance of the store. She steps quickly on the carpet that opens the electronic door, and walks in. *She* smiles. She has conquered fear again. Fear and a strange hypnotic desire, to speak to him. She knows her wish is obscene, unclean. She, the immaculate one, who on her wedding night stayed locked in the bathroom for two hours in dread. It was only when Peter promised he would not touch her, would even sleep on the floor that night, that she walked holding her robe tightly wrapped around her – wearing under her Pucci gown the security of panties. How long ago that seemed. Three children later it wasn't Peter's caresses she feared. It was her nameless desires. Cravings cravings. To dare obscenities. To walk nude in the street, even to touch to touch, to touch that thin obviously beggarly, maybe deranged man!

Today at least she has conquered the desire.

"Good morning, Mrs. Parsons. How are you today?"

It is Mr. Brown, the manager, who is a bit beggarly looking himself this morning, with his pale round face, his balding head, and that stupid ongoing smile.

"I'm fine, thank you."

"A beautiful morning, isn't it. A real storm last night. But the sun's out today."

She smiles, nods to Helene Williams, a short woman who always wears her frosted hair in an outrageous bun, as if she were trying to make herself a Victorian lady and yet hold on to some erroneously conceived contemporary look. Ann wears her hair straight. Peter loves it. He always says it glistens sun or no. She washes it every day, and the soft folds around her neck and face – perhaps it is the length – make her look, everyone says, like a sister of her ten-year-old daughter. The two of them do look alike. But how different they are. Peggy is funny. Her face is never still. She is always breaking into smiles or laughter. Ann is serious. People she knows call her "uptight" behind her back. She's overheard it! But she doesn't care. At least she doesn't have to, what is the word, "relate" to them. She can keep aloof. Keep her thoughts to herself, even those that aren't scary, obscene.

She likes the looks of the Granny Smith apples today, and almost forgets the thin man's stare as she selects some apples and puts them into a plastic bag. She counts six of the hard green fruit and is selecting a seventh when she feels a light touch upon her shoulder. She turns quickly. The touch is cold, icy, electrical, going into her veins, her flesh. She quivers as she looks upon the face of the thin man with his cigarette still dangling, that hairline mouth moving. She cannot make out a word he is saying. His lips are moving fast. Surely he is saying something? *What are you saying*, she asks, shaking yet desperately trying to understand him. His lips keep moving as he points to her handbag. *Mmmmmmmm*, he is mumbling. *Mmmmmm*.

"Oh, you want money?"

"Yyyyyy."

He is saying *yes*. She knows she should call the manager. But she doesn't. She opens her bag in the same frantic motion that earlier this morning she had used to pretend ignorance of the thin man's presence. This time she feels his piercing eyes staring into the bag. How much should she give him? She'll have to give him something. If she gives him something maybe the giving will be a connection that will be enough of a touch. Maybe she will no longer crave that obscene touch. She'll exorcise it by this ridiculous transaction.

Ann finds a dollar. The man's hand is outstretched. She is glad he is so tall. She needn't look up at him as she places the dollar bill into his hand. Her fingers touch his. Again that icy but electrical feeling seethes through her. She turns abruptly back to the fruit. How many apples has she put into the plastic bag? Is it six or seven? She automatically takes one two three four five six more. Her controlled counting reduces her panic. She buys nothing more. Walks up to the register. Pays for the apples to the puzzlement of the clerk who expects Ann's usual weekly overloaded shopping cart.

Ann manages to get to her car, turn on the ignition, drive out of the parking lot. It is only when she reaches home that her panic

panic subsides. But it is at least a half hour before she is able to open the car door, pick up her single supermarket purchase, turn the key and walk into her back hall. Has her transaction exorcised her desire? The answer is not in the excited welcoming bark of her slowly moving bloodhound.

The Room

YOU WALK THROUGH THE STREETS seeing buildings, shops, passersby but seeing nothing. Your eyes are steeled. You do not want to be caught touched by gesture, smile, caressing sounds. You walk not exactly as in a dream but as if walking were as natural as eating breakfast. A breakfast of cold cereal. A breakfast taken for granted, not that special breakfast of sausage and freshly baked croissants. Walking then through the streets, you hardly feel the Doberman pinscher rubbing against you nor hear the brutal sound of a burglar alarm go off as an electric current shifts in error. You walk with your tennis shoes, without sound, as they barely touch the pavement and hardly feel those cracks that were you alert would break up the monotony of your walk.

You've forgotten what city you are in. You feel it does not matter. You remember a train. You remember a plane too and indistinguishable clouds as your eyes carelessly looked out of the small window as you turned from your book for a moment. Once you used to look out of an airplane window, even out of such a one where the vista held only space, always noting with surprise that even clouds in their ceaseless movements created new forms so that looking out was exciting. Now you turned slowly from book to window, and then for many hours continued to read without regret, without feeling you had missed something. Nothing, you thought, had changed. Clouds are relentless, and the flight of the plane gave you through the window a feeling of void, of a mysterious space. That was enough to delight you.

You could, if you liked, have turned away from the book. The words were meaningless to you anyway. You read as if by habit. Was it a novel, a poem, a play?

As you look back on that trip, you do not know. Perhaps it was none of those. Perhaps it was Delacroix's *Journals* or Justin Kaplan's biography of Whitman. Or a new book on the brain or on some new physical theory about fractal dimensions. Words seem as senseless as your present walk and so your forgetting of that particular book on that particular plane ride seems unimportant.

You are a mere instrument, you feel, for the sensation of walking through streets of a city whose name remains unknown. You are not concerned about that ignorance either. Knowledge itself of towns, people, history is thinning out. Knowledge evaporates as television, cinema, radio become tools of enforced oblivion. Satellites, that enormous technological advance, seem to you to be other instruments to enable passersby to forget the word. The Word having fallen to the word, it cannot be missed anyway. Forgetfulness, oblivion, casualness are better weapons for the passerby who glances obliquely at store windows where bright colors, demonic mannikins (thin, emaciated, small-breasted, glaringly pink haired) stand still, outraged and outrageous. Silent mannikins stare. Passersby stare. You are merely one of the latter but your stare is short-lived as you walk these streets forgetting, forgetful, and carrying on with one foot after another as if a journey had its beginning in feet and ended with the same feet to condense variety into economy, to make feet alone the precious way, the way through rites de passage.

You discover that you have been holding your head down. You are bent, stooped. Are you old? Has your back broken through age or through a sense of defeat? Is the failure yours or the years? Can you lift those shoulders, can you hold your head high, level with the passersby or even higher? Can you lift your head toward the sky? You know that everywhere is sky. Cities have sky as well as towns and country.

As you experiment with lifting your head, there is a spasm of pain in your back that for the moment blocks your attempt. You are pleased that you have some kind of bravery left. Slowly you raise your head and it remains surprisingly on your shoulders, though a bit taut and heavy. You are now looking more or less like other passersby. Your head, that is, is on your shoulders, not drooping down, as you proceed along your walk on the street that is obviously in a city but a city whose name you do not know. You touch your arms. They are bare. You are glad to know that the weather is temperate. Perhaps it is even summer or perhaps this is a city in a tropical climate. You are relieved that you need not worry about luggage. If you are, even as you do not know, in a city having just arrived at least you will not be needing extra clothes. Your shirt will do. It will endure many washings. Socks, pants, underwear all seem, as you jerk yourself a little to make this discovery, adequate for a stay of a week or two, longer, if absolutely necessary.

As your hand searches in your right pocket, you feel a wallet and possibly an address book. You take out your wallet stopping near a telephone pole. The wallet has some bills and coins. You are curious to identify the currency. Hm. It looks like francs. You are too tired to investigate whether the francs are French or Swiss. You look around, see no mountains at least surrounding this city. You are probably in Paris, you think, and let it go at that – although you begin to try to overhear the language of the passersby. You think you hear something like *aujourd'hui, bien, je vous en prie*. But you are not sure. You wonder how long your lassitude will last, or is it your state of contentment. You may become hungry soon, so that at least one shop will have to be visited. A restaurant. You hope that will not be for some time.

Suddenly you feel a pat on your shoulder. Someone, a young woman, with very blond hair, shining as the sun plays with it, is saying to you with great joy: *Henri, Henri. You are here. You are here. You are here at last*. You find yourself embraced. You feel something happening to your body. Your blood seems warmer.

Is there a smile beginning to form on your lips? *Marie,* you are saying. Yet you hear yourself adding these words: "*Ne me dérange pas avant . . .*" Are you telling her not to disturb you? Marie, and it is Marie, is laughing at you. *Mon chéri,* she repeats, this time kissing you on your warm lips. You feel yourself being pushed along, her arm in yours. She is speaking quickly. You hardly hear her though the words *ma chambre* seem to stick in your ears. Also *mon hôtel mon hôtel* and *rue Jacob rue Jacob.* She is laughing excitedly now. And you are laughing too. You suddenly find yourself stopping. You have taken her in your arms. She is saying *mais non* as you kiss her passionately on the lips. She is laughing. You are both standing still. Ah, *mon chéri,* you hear. You are remembering vividly now. You are climbing up some stairs. You are holding hands. She is laughing. You are laughing. She is holding a key. She is opening a door. You follow her into the room.